SHANE PEACOCK

LAST MESSAGE

ORCA BOOK PUBLISHERS

Library and Archives Canada Cataloguing in Publication

Peacock, Shane
Last message / Shane Peacock.
(Seven (the series))

Issued also in an electronic format.
ISBN 978-1-55469-935-3

I. Title. II. Series: Seven the series
PS8581.E234L37 2012   jc813'.54   C2012-902580-1

First published in the United States, 2012
Library of Congress Control Number: 2012938219

Summary: At the request of his late grandfather, Adam flies to France
in order to perform three difficult tasks that involve a lost painting,
a famous book and a forbidden cave.

*Orca Book Publishers is dedicated to preserving the environment and has
printed this book on Forest Stewardship Council® certified paper.*

Orca Book Publishers gratefully acknowledges the support for its publishing
programs provided by the following agencies: the Government of Canada
through the Canada Book Fund and the Canada Council for the Arts,
and the Province of British Columbia through the BC Arts Council
and the Book Publishing Tax Credit.

Design by Teresa Bubela
Cover photography by Getty Images
Author photo by Kevin Kelly

ORCA BOOK PUBLISHERS
PO Box 5626, Stn. B
Victoria, BC Canada
V8R 6S4

ORCA BOOK PUBLISHERS
PO Box 468
Custer, WA USA
98240-0468

www.orcabook.com
Printed and bound in Canada.

16 15 14 13 • 6 5 4 3

To Susan and Jackson Peacock,
best of friends

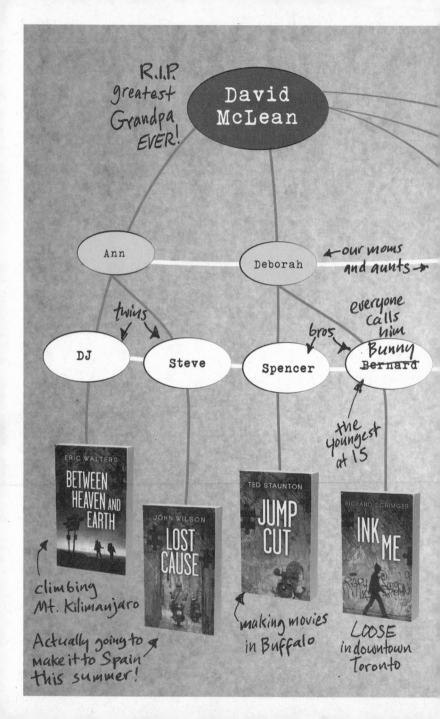

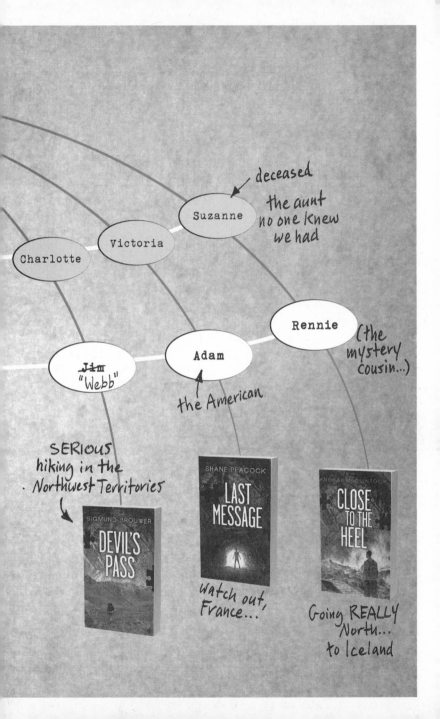

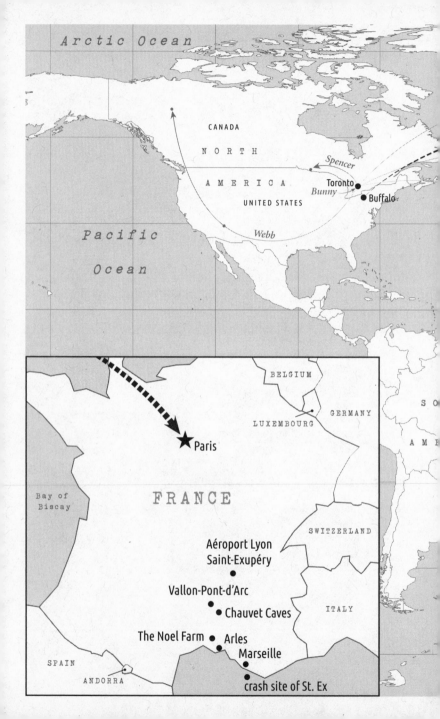

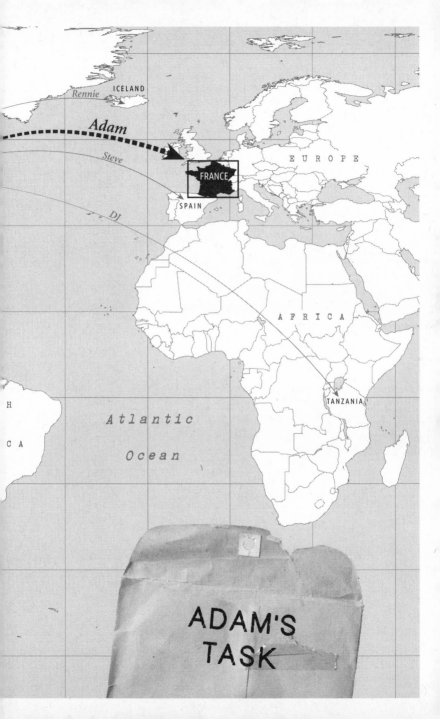

"Go and look again at the roses."

—ANTOINE DE SAINT-EXUPÉRY,
THE LITTLE PRINCE

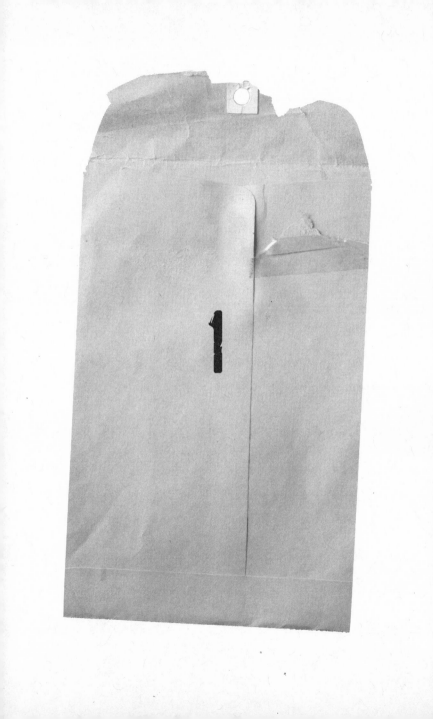

ONE

MATTERS OF CONSEQUENCE

"He'll never amount to much."

That's what he said. In fact, it was the *last* thing he said about me.

I tried not to resent him as I sat with my mother and father in the gloomy, wood-paneled room in his lawyer's office in Toronto, Canada, fifty floors up in the clouds. It wasn't the appropriate time to resent him, not at all. I very much doubted that anyone else in the room had even remotely similar feelings. He was dead, after all, freshly flown off on his final adventure into the skies, so fit and "with it" that we were all shocked to hear of his death…at age ninety-two.

My aunts, one uncle and five cousins—most of the McLean family, in fact—were gathered around too, restless in big leather chairs. I assumed they were thinking about how great he had been. They were right. I held my bottom lip tightly, though I think it was quivering a little. All three of my aunts had Kleenex in hand, and their faces were pretty red. My Uncle Jerry sat stoically, his mouth in a straight line, and my cousins, all boys, were looking down at the floor or up at the ceiling, not making eye contact with anyone, likely deathly afraid they might start to cry. Even DJ, the oldest grandson (actually only a few minutes older than his twin Steve, but much more mature) who liked to think of himself as kind of the leader of our generation, seemed a little shaky. I think Canadians are a bit wimpy anyway, despite what they can do on the ice.

Mom and Dad looked different. They're really strong people, just like Grandpa, and it showed in their faces. We were the American branch of the family, maybe that was why. We had converted Mom, who was born up here. She was her father's favorite; everyone knew that, so you'd think she'd be the most upset. But you wouldn't know it if you saw her today.

She was holding herself together, looking as calm as I'm sure Grandpa was (Canadian, but no wimp) when he flew one of his missions over France, or as Dad looked the day he landed his American Airlines Airbus at Kennedy Airport on *one* engine, with three hundred passengers on board.

The blinds were drawn in the room, keeping the bright Canadian morning out. Other than the odd sniffle, no one was saying anything. An old, upright clock ticked loudly in a corner.

It wasn't that I wasn't sad. I was. And it wasn't that I didn't love my grandfather. I definitely did. I knew I would miss him hugely, we all would. You'd have to be a robot not to. But I just wished he hadn't said that about me. And I wished it wasn't the last thing I heard out of his mouth. I had enough issues without that…though I think I've hidden them pretty well.

The McLean family was used to getting together for much happier occasions. Grandpa was always the center of things, even when he was really old… just like today, when you think of it. He never shut up and he never stopped moving. He had a story for and about everything and anything, and they were always well told. But then again, he had a lot to

3

work with—if you wanted to know about being shot at over Nazi-occupied France, sky-high adventures in Iceland, or flying dangerous sorties in Eastern Africa, he was your guy.

I remember the last time we were all in one place, just last summer up near his cottage in the Muskoka Lakes district in the province of Ontario, where lots of movie stars had huge holiday homes. I heard Tom Cruise had property up that way, and (of course) loads of hockey stars summered in those parts too. The cottage was a special McLean place, and we'd had all kinds of fun there over the years. But the highlight for just about everyone but me was the day a few years back when we met in a field near the lake so Grandpa could fly his airplane in and take his grandsons up for a ride. It was one of the last times he flew—one of the final missions in his incredible career. I, uh, remember it all too well.

I threw up. Barfed all over the inside of his precious big bird. And, of course, I was the only one who performed that particular sacrilege. I think I covered up well though—said I hadn't been feeling the best all day. I could be wrong, but it seemed like all the other guys aced the thing with flying colors

4

(so to speak). I came down as white as the door of his plane.

Problem is, it isn't supposed to be that way with me. That was why that "He'll never amount to much" thing was really hard to deal with. I'm the son of his favorite daughter; I was given his second name; I was the one he flew all night to see in Buffalo on the day I was born (which just happened to be his birthday too); I'm the one about whom he whispered to Mom, "This one is precious."

It would be different if I were a loser. But I'm not. I'm on the football team and the hockey team (ready for my Canuck cousins at the rink any day), and I've got a nice-looking girlfriend. My marks are okay too. But that's the problem. *Okay.* Everything is just okay with me—strong safety in football, not quarterback; fifth in scoring in hockey, not first; barely on the Honor Roll, not top of the class. And the girl I really want—the one all of us guys at McKinley High want—the goddess Vanessa, with that killer body and blond hair that seems to blow in the wind even when she is just standing at her locker, barely knows I exist. I sometimes feel guilty about my interest in her, since it's probably just about looks and because everyone wants her. I know I can be insecure sometimes, and it makes me act like a jerk. But I feel like I have so much to live up to. I'm tall for my age and have Grandpa's dark looks, so I have something to work with. You'd think I'd do better. I'm Adam McLean Murphy, grandson of a legendary war hero, son of John Murphy, the famous airline pilot and decorated Gulf War hero, and Victoria McLean, who ran the 400 meters for Canada in the Olympics and made her father proud. And I'm just "okay."

In my opinion, that isn't good enough.

He'll never amount to much. As usual, Grandpa was right on the money. If he'd said that when I was ten or twelve, that would have been different, but it was just last month, last bloody month. I've only got a couple of years of high school left! It feels like the die has been cast.

❖

The door opened and in came Grandpa's lawyer, dressed in a very unfashionable suit and tie. It looked like he'd bought it at a Target store or some Canadian equivalent.

"Good afternoon," he said with a forced smile. It was quickly obvious that he had been under David McLean's spell too. He began by mumbling something about it being a sad day and how much he had revered Grandpa and couldn't believe he was dead, despite Grandpa being a lot older. It was as if he figured the great man would live forever.

Actually, he *will* live forever, I thought, up there in the sky, looming over us all like a giant shadow.

His funeral had been very difficult. Everyone was really broken up. It was so hard to believe that he was lying there in that open coffin, actually still for more than a second. I could barely look at him. I was overwhelmed with both sadness and anger. It wasn't a good scene...inside my head.

The lawyer started droning on in legal terms about Grandpa's will. *Blah, blah, blah.* I just wanted to get out of there and move on—all of this stuff was for our parents' benefit. And I was *still* feeling too guilty about not being sad, or at least, not sad enough. I wanted to wrap this up.

But on and on he went, speaking about "assets" being "liquidated and dispersed to the heirs." Big surprise! If I hadn't been packed full of conflicting feelings,

7

I would have fallen asleep. I began thinking about Vanessa: those tight jeans she wears, those form-fitting sweaters.

But then the lawyer actually said something interesting. He stopped for a moment before he said it, as if he had a momentous message to convey. It got my attention.

"A sum of money," he said, his voice dropping lower, "a rather substantial sum, has been put aside to fund an undertaking...or I should say, *seven* undertakings."

Seven undertakings? There are seven aunts and uncles, including Webb's stepdad, who wasn't here. The twins' dad had died a long time ago.

But there was something about the way he said it. He'd raised his eyebrows and emphasized the word. But why would Grandpa fund some sort of mysterious project for *each* of his daughters and sons-in-law? Wouldn't it be better to do it by family—the four families? Why would Dad, for example, take on one thing and Mom another? It didn't make much sense. And what could these *undertakings* (which sounded like something funeral directors did) possibly be? Something strange was going on; Grandpa had something up his sleeve. I looked around at my cousins. There were six of *us*, not seven—five Canucks and a Yankee.

"This is without a doubt one of the most unusual clauses that I have ever been asked to put in a will." The lawyer shook his head and smiled.

Now he had my *full* attention.

But then he said he couldn't share the details with everyone. It seemed like a polite way of telling the grandchildren that secrets were going to be kept from us. There was an eruption of protest. The lawyer tried to silence everyone by continuing to speak. But what he had to say didn't help at all.

"Some people will have to leave the room prior to the undertakings being read."

One cousin, good old Steve, snorted and began to make a bigger fuss. That was when the rest of my cousins—Webb, Spencer, Bunny (I know, it's a lame name, but he's a weirdo and he likes it, and I might too, if my name was *Bernard*) and even the holier-than-the-rest-of-us DJ—started complaining more too. At first there were just a few comments; then things got louder and all hell broke loose. They really gave it to the lawyer about "not going anywhere." The parents didn't help. As they tried to calm their kids, they muttered a few things about this not making sense.

But not *my* parents: Mom and Dad were the only ones who didn't offer any sort of protest. They were often the best-behaved people in any room, and usually the best-looking too. It really ticked me off.

I wished I was as relaxed as them. My stomach was churning. Something about this had begun to worry me, *really* worry me. I looked at the lawyer and saw his eyes twinkling. I had a distinct feeling that this wasn't what it seemed. Our grandfather was pulling strings—again—and we were all about to be surprised, big-time.

"I need to have everyone *except* the six grand-sons," said the lawyer with a pause and a barely detectable smile, "leave the room."

TWO
SECRETS

Once all the parents were out of the room, a miracle happened. The lawyer directed our attention to a TV in a cabinet, pressed a button on a remote control, and suddenly Grandpa was alive again. He looked out at us from a television screen, saying that he loved us and telling us that life was a journey. When he talked about our grandmother, Vera, tears came to his eyes. She was an amazing lady (of course) who had died long before any of us were born. He had raised his four accomplished daughters on his own. As he talked, he was funny and crusty and brilliant (of course) and I missed him like crazy. I also wanted to yell at him, tell him he was wrong about me. His ever-present black beret was on his head, making him look more worldly than any man his age had a right to be. It said that he knew Europe like the back of his hand, had been everywhere else too, done everything, and looked down upon the planet from above—the Picasso of adventure.

Then he said something weird. He mentioned his "wonderful, incredible" grandsons. But that wasn't what was so strange. It was what he said after that. He called us his "*seven* blessings."

I looked around at the five other guys. DJ raised his hands at me to indicate that he didn't know what Grandpa was on about; Steve made a little circle in the air with his hand, right near his head, as if to say the great David McLean had lost it. The others just sat there with puzzled expressions.

I started thinking: *seven* grandsons, *seven* undertakings. Almost the moment I thought that, Grandpa confirmed that the undertakings were for us. My eyes snapped up to meet his. Every one of my cousins leaned forward in their comfy leather chairs.

"In the possession of my lawyer are some envelopes..." Grandpa continued.

I didn't hear much else. My mind was racing.

When his image vanished, we sat there in silence.

Then the lawyer dropped a final bomb on us. He told us that Grandpa had had a brief relationship with a woman long after his wife died, and recently discovered that he had another daughter, who had a son. There were indeed *seven* grandsons.

As we tried to take that in, we were handed our undertakings, seven assignments. Some of the envelopes were bigger and thicker than others, but each had nothing but our names on the front. It was as if we were CIA operatives. I glanced around at the other guys again. Most of them seemed pretty calm, more curious than concerned.

But not me.

I knew what was *really* happening. David McLean was testing us from beyond the grave, each and every one of his boys, his mighty grandsons. This had the smell of a competition. And if we were going to be tested, I *had* to do well. *Very* well. *Better* than well.

I had to win.

THREE

TESTS

As we drove home to Buffalo that night, it was quiet in the suv. Mom was at the wheel, going top speed as usual, and Dad was fast asleep in the passenger seat. Or at least, he seemed to be. She appeared preoccupied, as if she were contemplating her next big real-estate deal. One of the top ten realtors in New York State last year—that was Victoria McLean Murphy. But I knew they were acting. I doubted he was really asleep or that she was thinking about anything other than the four items on my lap, all from one of the biggest packages my grandfather had left for any of us—three large manila envelopes and one small white one.

I didn't blame Mom and Dad. Who wouldn't have been curious? Grandpa had such a sense of drama. All the parents had been called back into the lawyer's office after we'd seen the video. Things had been explained to them. But not everything. And they knew it.

It was me who broke the silence in the car. It was nice to have held it for so long, controlling things, in charge of my parents for once.

"I'm sure you are wondering exactly what happened in there."

"Pardon me, dear?" asked Mom.

"Did you say something, buddy?"

Nice try, guys. "I'll tell you."

"No need," Mom said.

"No, it's okay," I said.

"Well, if you insist."

"I do."

"You don't need to explain everything." Dad smiled.

"I won't."

"What do you mean, you won't?" asked Mom, a little sternly.

"Because I can't; that's part of the deal. You need to know some things, and I can't tell you others."

I looked down at the envelopes. The larger ones were numbered one to three. I'd sliced open the first the minute we'd gotten into the car. There was a long letter inside. I'd read the first two pages but then stopped. It was almost too much to take in. At the beginning, my grandfather had written that I could share some of its contents, just those first pages, with my parents. I'd noticed Mom eyeing me in the rear-view mirror a couple of times while I'd been reading, glancing away when I'd looked up at her; and Dad had even cocked an eye in the mirror, pretending that he was turning in his sleep. I'd never known him to snooze in the car before.

"Well, what *can* you share with us, Master Murphy?" I'm sure he was annoyed that Grandpa had told me to withhold information from him and Mom.

"Well, you know about the seventh grandson."

"Yes, dear," said Mom. "Your grandfather told us a while ago."

"He gave us all tasks."

Dad kept looking out the window, as if he were only mildly interested. "Are those the undertakings that the lawyer was talking about?"

"What do you mean by tasks?" asked Mom.

"Well, they're adventures, assignments, tests—however you want to put it—for all seven grandsons."

"I don't get it," said Dad.

"Grandpa said there were things he hadn't accomplished, if you can believe it, things he wanted to do during his life, but never did. Things left undone."

"That *is* hard to believe," said Mom.

"So?" asked Dad, turning around and looking at me.

"We—my cousins and I—are going to do them for him. Or at least try to."

There was just the sound of the car moving along the highway for a few seconds.

"I hope these aren't dangerous things," said Mom.

"You're both supposed to go with me."

"And help you do what?" asked Dad.

"You don't help me. You just go with me."

"Okay," said Mom. "Would it be too much to ask *where* we are going? How long will the drive be?"

"To France."

"France?" they both sputtered.

"This summer, to a place called Marseille."

"The *l*s are silent, dear. You should know that."

Mom had made me take private French lessons once a week from the time I was about seven. It was

17

her way of keeping me Canadian, or so she said. Not that she was even remotely bilingual herself. She hadn't even been any good at ordering lunch in Montreal when we visited the French-Canadian province of Quebec last year. I didn't listen much to the woman who taught me. It wasted my free time. And there weren't any marks to be had either.

"Okay, Mar-say," I said with my best French accent.

"That's on the southern coast," said Dad. "Your grandfather flew reconnaissance missions in that area in the Second World War."

Like I hadn't been told that a million times, right from the lips of the war hero himself! Iceland, East Africa, France, the tales were endless. Not that I hated hearing them: they were actually pretty wicked, but I could have done with fewer renditions, despite the fact that they came in useful whenever I wanted Vanessa to give me a moment of her time. She really had no interest in talking to *me*. (Not that most sophomore girls talked much to sophomore boys anyway, unless you were somehow supercool.) She'd only listen to me if she heard me talking about Grandpa's time in France or Dad's exploits in the Gulf War. "It's so romantic," she said once. "They're like heroes from another time." She was a very proud American and often wore jeans that had a stars-and-stripes patch sewn on just above her butt. Her dad had been in the National Guard and had about fifty *Support Our Troops, America First!* and *Peace Through Superior Firepower* decals on their car. He was an executive of some sort who worked for the Republican Party in our district. I remember the day Dad showed up at school in his United Airlines pilot's uniform. Vanessa came right over to talk to us and stayed for a while. And the time Grandpa dropped by to pick me up after class, she immediately asked to be introduced to him. "So, *you* are David McLean," she said, her voice rising a little. "I've heard so much about you!" Of course, he regaled her with some pretty dramatic tales. He had a way with the ladies, right to the end. She told me later that he didn't look a day over sixty.

It didn't hurt that Grandpa had actually done his flying for the US Air Force during the Second World War, drawn there because he had some American business connections, signed up a little late and liked the sort of firepower and advanced technology we had in our planes. (David McLean always liked to go as fast as he could.) He'd had a grandfather who was a US citizen, which he said helped him get in, but in those days just about anyone who wanted to enlist was apparently welcome. Vanessa thought it was awfully moving that a Canadian would fight under the US flag and then "be so brave!" Little did she know that he wasn't the biggest fan of "you Yanks," as he liked to call us.

My girlfriend, Shirley, who is in tenth grade too but pretty down-to-earth and cool with dating a guy in her year, didn't fawn over Dad or Grandpa at all. Shirley was nice and polite every time I had her over to our place. She was great, and I really liked her. She was an excellent friend and quite good-looking, but she didn't light up a room like Vanessa. If the Big V had been in my house or in my bedroom like Shirley's been a couple of times, my place would have been glowing. I had kissed Shirley, more than once and with some feeling, with Mom and Dad just down the hall. It was pretty good. But sometimes I imagined it with Vanessa, and man, that just sent me over the moon. If that ever happened, even once, or even almost once, I would have tried to commit it to memory—*exactly* how she smelled, how she felt, how she looked in my room at that moment.

✦

"I'll read you the first page," I said, turning my attention back to Mom and Dad.

"Are you sure you should even do that? Maybe you should keep it all to yourself," said Mom, letting her displeasure show in her voice. I could understand. Her father was excluding her from something that was important to him.

"Just listen. This is pretty incredible."

Dear Adam,

By now you have seen me blathering on in the video about how much I love you all. Sorry about that. But I DO love you. And I hope you love me too and that our bond will grow even more as the years go by, especially after you have done the things I am asking you to attempt in these letters. If you decide to take on what I am suggesting, you will go on a journey into my past and into my mind. It will help you with your future.

I spent a long time thinking about what I wanted you to do, Adam. I've come up with something very important, very private. It is fitting that I'm asking you, of all my grandsons, to do it. It will show you a side of me that you've never seen before, a side that I'm ashamed of.

This is your task, sir.

Actually, it's three tasks, of ascending difficulty. I'm not sure you can accomplish any of them, but I'd like you to at least try the first one. It is a momentous assignment in itself, a mission that may be too much for you, that I may not have the right to ask of you. Its details are in the following pages. If you cannot complete it, there will be no shame and I (up in heaven or down below or wherever the hell I am) will completely understand. But if, somehow, you are able to find the courage and imagination to do it, you can then go on to the second task, outlined in envelope number two.

Though I trust in your abilities, I truly doubt that you can complete the second adventure—it is beyond difficult, even more challenging than the first.

Assignment three is in envelope three. Finishing it, I must say, is virtually impossible.

You may only open one envelope at a time, after the task in the preceding one has been accomplished. And you may only unseal the last envelope—the small white one—in the unlikely event you complete the first three assignments. If you stall at a level, you must end your adventures there. Destroy the contents of the envelopes you haven't read. I will rest uneasily if you do not obey these rules.

All your expenses will be covered. You should start your journey as soon as you can.

Here's how to begin:

Fly to Marseille, France, with your parents. My lawyer will arrange and pay for your flights. Your parents are to book a room in the nicest hotel in the city and have the holiday of their lives in the south of France. They are to make themselves available to you by cell phone at all times. But they are not to help you in ANY way with your tasks.

Once they are settled, you are to travel, on your own, half an hour north of Marseille to the beautiful old town of Arles and take up residence in a hotel there. This will be your headquarters as you pursue your adventures.

Please keep the next pages to yourself.

There was silence in the car when I finished.

It was curious to me that I was to start my assignment in France. Of all the stories Grandpa told, he was most vague about his experiences in that part of Europe. He used to give us all sorts of details about his other adventures, but when it came to France and the Second World War, his tales weren't as personal. He mostly spoke of the mind-blowing planes he flew and how his comrades survived dangerous situations. Usually, all he said about himself was that that he had been shot at while flying over France (he described it really well—it sounded terrifying) and that his plane had been hit hard more than once. But those stories seemed to end rather abruptly, petering out without resolutions, him still in the sky, never suffering further trouble, nor even limping back to his base. Mom said that, like many veterans, he found it difficult to talk in exact terms about the horrors he may have seen. Now I was wondering if there was a lot more to it than that.

"Well, that's interesting, *very* interesting," said Mom. "Another 'side' of himself? And what's he 'ashamed' of?"

"Indeed," said Dad. "I knew Dave probably kept some state secrets, some inside air-force things, but I didn't think he was hiding any big personal ones."

"Well, it appears he was—more than one," snapped Mom.

But I was barely listening. I held the next pages in my hands. There were quite a few of them. I wasn't surprised at that—Grandpa always had a lot to say. I picked up the first one and began to devour its contents.

FOUR
THE FIRST ENVELOPE

This is difficult to even write. Don't EVER show this to anyone. Burn it when you are done, whether you accomplish the assignment or not. You know a tiny bit of this, but not all of it, not the important parts. I will tell it from the beginning, leaving everything in this time. Here goes:

During the war, I was stationed on the island of Corsica in the Mediterranean Sea. We flew secret reconnaissance missions over southern France from there, over the area then called Vichy. The French hadn't exactly set up a Pittsburgh Steelers defense against the Nazis at the beginning of the war and got their butts kicked quickly. Hitler and his psychos overran their country in a heartbeat. And a whole whack of the French just kind of let him do it and then made an alliance with him with the cooperation of France's greatest general from World War I, an ass named Pétain. Together, they agreed that a big chunk of southern France would be run by the French, a sort of "Free France" or "Free Zone." Of course, that was a joke, since it was really a Nazi-dominated area, and believe me, there was nothing "free" about that.

It was a pleasant place for most of the war, and the French who lived there just kind of went about their business, far from the battlegrounds, ignorant of what Hitler was doing to the Jews and the violence he was perpetrating on us and the Allied Forces all over Europe. (Canadians, of course, were in the big fight from the get-go; then you Americans came on board a few years later, after the Allies had held the fort and suffered terrible losses, and you "won the war for the world," as you guys like to say.)

But there was an underground war going on in Vichy too. Not all the French were avoiding the conflict. A significant number were very brave and became members of the French Resistance, who fought the bad guys tooth and nail, secretly, risking their lives by helping spies and committing guerrilla warfare against the Vichy government, its military, German soldiers and officials.

Then there were the REALLY bad guys: French Nazis who formed a militia called the Milice. You may have heard of the Gestapo and the SS, the German state police known for their black uniforms and skull-and-crossbones badges? Well, the Milice were just as evil, maybe worse. They hunted the French Resistance fighters like dogs, and when they caught them or anyone else who helped the Allies or Jews, they tortured them and murdered them without thinking twice. Everyone in southern France was terrified of them.

By late in the war, the tide was turning against the Nazis, and by early June of 1944 we'd landed in Normandy on the French coast across from England—that was the big D-Day invasion. But we still needed to know more about the enemy, where their strengths and weaknesses were, so we could overrun them, sweep across France and into Germany, and take them out for good. In Vichy (by then directly operated by the anxious Germans) things were getting bad for the Nazis and their supporters. They and the Milice knew the end was coming, and they were all desperate, which made them even more vicious.

This is where I come in.

There I was one night, flying over southern France in June of 1944 on a reconnaissance mission, gliding as quietly as possible, getting low but not too low, taking aerial photographs of enemy locations, looking down upon the land of the Milice and the Nazis.

Then someone put a round of anti-aircraft bullets into my engine. It was a funny thing. Everything was quiet until they hit. Suddenly, there was a sound like big mosquitoes coming up from the ground and in an instant everything was on fire. The plane did a nosedive and I couldn't stop it. I was scared, but I did what I had to do, what I'd been trained to do. In seconds I was out of the aircraft and into the sky, just me and my parachute.

Down I went, down toward the land of evil. It was just about dusk, the perfect time to get pictures and yet not be observed particularly well. I couldn't see much below me, just fields.

I knew I was somewhere over Arles.

"Learning anything new?" asked Dad.

"Yeah, a bit. It's pretty good."

"Good?" asked Mom.

I looked out the window. We were somewhere between Hamilton and Niagara Falls.

"Just let me read."

I landed in an open field, which wasn't a good thing. I had noticed an area nearby that was full of trees—turned out later to be grapevines—and tried to steer toward it, but couldn't quite manage it. We hadn't spent much time on parachute training, so I hit the ground at a pretty good rate, and awkwardly, and busted my ankle.

I figured I was a goner. As I was rolling around in the grass, trying to gather up my chute, I was half expecting to see a bloodthirsty contingent of Milice coming at me, lights blazing, guns trained. And sure enough, within seconds, someone appeared. He was alone, but armed. He had an ax in his hand and he looked at me with what appeared to be terror. His eyes were almost bulging out of his head.

At first I could tell that he wasn't sure what to do: yell that the enemy had landed, kill me or save me. He chose the last option, motivated by a goodness deep within him and a hatred of what Hitler had done to his country and to others. He was an angel. Jean Noel was his name. John Christmas. And when he appeared, I received the greatest gift of my life.

He was as strong as an ox, with hard-calloused working hands on him like mitts on a gorilla, and he dragged me into the vineyard, out of sight. He knelt down, his face up close to mine and spoke in a whisper, his eyes still fearful.

"Jean Noel," he said. "Okay. Okay?"

"David Adam McLean, US Air Force."

He returned to the open field, stuffed my parachute under his arm, came back, got me to my feet, braced me with a shoulder and walked me the five miles to his home, looking back with almost every other step.

I learned later that he had been clearing dead vines with his ax that night, toiling extra hours for a rich Nazi sympathizer. His own tiny farm was about two acres, on which he and his wife Yvette kept about a dozen chickens, a few pigs, two cows and a workhorse. He plowed an acre and a half with that horse, and used the poor beast for transportation whenever he hitched her to his little wagon to go to market in Arles, about ten miles away. Their house was made of stone, maybe five hundred years old, smaller than your garage. It had a low ceiling and just two rooms, one that served as their kitchen-living-and-dining room and another where they all slept. They had two small children, a boy and a girl. When we arrived, Yvette, a pretty lady, a little plump and wearing a dirty apron over her tattered blue-flowered dress, put her hands on her cheeks and began to cry. "Non, non, non, non, non! Non, Jean!" She kept her voice low but she was still screaming. She pulled the two children close to her.

But Jean had made up his mind, and that is why you, Adam, are alive today. Because the Milice would have killed me the minute they saw me. No, that isn't correct. They would have tortured me first. And they would have tortured and killed Jean too, and done worse to Yvette.

The stone-floored and stone-walled room felt damp, but there was a lovely smell of a wood fire and wonderful home-cooked food in the air. I could see a butter churner and a loom in the cramped quarters. Jean immediately threw my parachute into their fire.

So, that was where I lived for the next month, as my ankle healed. Not exactly in the house though. After they had quickly fed me stew and homemade bread, mixed with a little cheap red wine, Jean checked that it was safe outside and then took me just a few strides to his little barn. It was made of stone too and housed the horse, two cows, the few pigs and those chickens. I would get to know them well, know exactly when the rooster crowed each morning, and learn to live with the smell of manure in that damp, dark place. He helped me over the fence that contained the pigs and we slopped a few paces through their cramped pen, past the big sow and her piglets and then over the next fence, this one covered with webs of fine wire, into the tiny area at the back where the chickens were.

31

What Jean did then made me more than a little tense. He grabbed a spade and started digging a grave. Or at least that was what it looked like. We were right at the back of the chicken pen. The ground didn't have much grass on it—the chickens had seen to that—but the earth was thick and chocolate-colored. Jean set to work. And when Jean worked at anything, he went whole hog. He put his back into it, as well as his huge hands and arms, and about ten minutes later had dug a shallow grave about six feet long and two or three feet deep.

It was for me.

He motioned for me to lie in it. At that very moment we heard the hum of an engine—it sounded like a truck—coming up the little road toward his house.

"Vite!" he cried, and I got down and he began to throw the dirt and sod onto me. His eyes had grown to the great size they had been when he first saw me—the fear had returned. I lay flat and let him cover me. We could hear men getting out of the truck and then entering the house without knocking; we heard angry, accusatory voices and Yvette's frightened one-word answers. Then we heard footsteps approaching the barn.

"Anything interesting?" asked Mom.

"Mom, just let me read!"

Jean worked frantically, patting down the sod over me. He reached into the straw, found a large hollow strand and handed it to me, motioning for me to put it in my mouth and hold it up. I did. Then he mimed closing my eyes and mouth and began to throw the dirt, then sod, right over my face. I gasped, closed my nostrils with two fingers and breathed through the straw. I could hear the voices calling out his name, more straw being tossed on top of my grave and then several empty wooden feed buckets jammed into place near my head and inches from the end of the pen, so the straw that I breathed through was between them and the wall. The chickens wouldn't step on it or peck at it there.

Then I heard the spade being flung away and Jean stepping over the wired fence into the pigpen, addressing his visitors as he went.

"Je suis ici."

"Ah, Monsieur Noel, bon soir."

It was a sickly sweet voice, with about as much sincerity as the devil might have.

"Bon soir," said Jean.

"Vous admirez les cochons, je pense."

"Non, je travaille."

"Nous recherchons un Américain. Un aviateur, un pilote, un ennemi de la France, un diable. L'avez-vous vu?"

"Un Américain? Non."

Jean's voice was shaky. That wasn't good.

They began to search the barn. By that time, the chickens were scratching around on the ground right over me. I tried not to breathe through my nose, into which I had thrust my fingers. It wasn't easy. But you can do that sort of thing when your life depends on it. The Milice men didn't come near me. They obviously didn't fancy entering the pigpen, didn't want to dirty their gleaming jackboots in the manure or be run at by the big sow. Moments later they were gone, but then I heard them smashing things in the house, shouting something about the fireplace, yelling at the Noels. Yvette cried loudly and her children screamed as something— a hammer maybe, or an ax—whacked their stone floors.

But the Noels revealed nothing...for me.

And they stayed quiet for the better part of the month. Yvette resented me at first, but in a week or two she grew less frightened and then doted on me like a sister. I spent most of every day in the barn, often buried in the grave, but she would bring me breakfast, lunch and dinner, wonderful French peasant food of homemade bread and tasty soup and chicken and eggs and sometimes even her sweet homemade pastry. Yvette couldn't read or write, and neither could Jean, but they were the nicest human beings I ever met.

Sometimes, when it got dark, they would even sneak me into the house to play a game of checkers or so we could converse in our fractured way, using lots of hand signals, Jean sitting at the little front window with the shutters open wide on another warm Provençal summer evening, watching for any movement along the dirt road toward his house.

And all the time I was there, at least after the second day, I felt terrible. I felt as guilty as if I were helping Hitler.

"Guilty?" I said out loud.

"Did you say 'guilty,' buddy?"

"No."

"Yes, you did."

"Don't lie," said Mom.

"I guess I did, yeah, but I didn't mean to. I was just surprised."

"Surprised?"

"This is getting a little weird. Just let me read."

Why, you ask, did I feel guilty?

Because of what happened the second morning I was in the barn. It has stayed with me for the rest of my life.

I had been so frightened, so emotional that first day that I hadn't moved an inch throughout the night. I just lay there, breathing through the straw, too anxious to sleep. In the morning, when Jean came and uncovered me and gave me breakfast, I was exhausted. We were both so scared that he covered me up again. I must have slept for about fifteen hours after that. I had lost my watch in the crash, and the Noels told time by the sun. I woke in terror, thinking I had been buried alive. But then I remembered where I was and pushed myself up and out. I sat there, leaning against the wall, looking at the chickens, who turned their heads in their jerky fashion so they could gawk at me with their slow-witted eyes. The pigs snorted and watched too, peeking through the gaps in their pen. I looked at them and they looked back. But the sow occasionally glanced up and beyond me, and when I turned to see what seemed to be catching her attention, I saw a crude painting nailed to a board above me, with a thin film of grime on it. It was hard to tell what it depicted, but it had a great deal of yellow in it, great slashes of glowing yellow, contrasted with startling reds and oranges and a blue as bright as the French sky. I couldn't turn away. I stood up and brushed the grime off the painting and at that instant I could clearly see what I was looking at, and I nearly fell facedown into the manure.

I knew what the painting was.

"What? What was it?" I said out loud.

"You are doing it again," said Dad, "and it's pretty annoying."

"Either tell us what he is saying or be quiet," added Mom.

"I'll be quiet. It's just that…you'd understand if you were reading it."

"Well, clearly, we are not."

Your great-grandfather McLean may have been a farmer, toiling hard on his land in southern Ontario, but he made sure all his children knew about literature and art. He often took us to galleries in the city and, as you know, turned me into a lifelong fan of the great artists. I knew then, and I know now, when a painting is worth a fortune.

I know a master's original when I see one. I know a Vincent Van Gogh.

That was what was hanging in that pigpen in Arles.

"Holy crap!"

Mom and Dad both turned around and looked at me. She even took her hands off the steering wheel for a moment. I glanced up at them, muttered "Sorry" and then went back to the letter and continued to read.

37

The Noels were about as ignorant of the world as a young family could be in 1944. They had no running water, no electricity, and had certainly never been anywhere near an art gallery.

My mind began to race. How could a Van Gogh sunflower be in this pigpen? How could this be? Then I thought about what I knew of the great artist.

He was as famous for his insanity as he was for his genius. I had heard the story of him cutting off his ear. I tried to remember what else I knew about him. And then I remembered—Van Gogh had lived in southern France...in Arles!

A shiver went through me.

I quickly thought of what else I knew. After the gruesome self-mutilation, he had been put into an insane asylum nearby. All his friends in the area were ordinary people, some of them peasants. They pitied him and often accepted his "horrible" paintings—the worthless works of a lunatic—as gifts.

The first day the Noels had me into their home, I tried to ask them about the painting. It was hard going. I didn't learn much. But as the days passed, Jean was able to convey to me that his father had given him the painting, that it had been in his grandfather's woodshed for many years before the turn of the century, and that he had been told that it had been done by a crazy man with red hair and beard, who knew his

38

grandfather. Once or twice, Jean picked up a pencil and paper and drew what he was trying to say. That helped with details. Apparently, Jean's grandfather had been a postman in the area and a bit of a drinker who loved to spend evenings in the Arles cafés, making friends. Jean always laughed when he turned to the subject of the painting. He mimed how it was so bad he had wanted to throw it out, but had put it up in the pen to amuse the pigs and chickens, and lo and behold, they seemed to like it. In fact, ever since it had been hung there, the chickens had laid bigger eggs and the pigs had tasted even better than before. Jean never laughed louder than when he told that story.

I tried not to show my astonishment. I didn't know what to say, so I said nothing.

Then I made the decision that shamed me for the rest of my life.

I decided to steal the Van Gogh.

"What!?"

"Okay, Adam, stop it. Just stop it."

I knew that the Van Gogh, sitting in their pigpen, grime-covered and hidden from the world, was worth a whole lot of money. And in a few years, in decades, it might be worth millions.

I lay awake at night in my grave, rationalizing. The painting was small for a Van Gogh, small enough that I could conceal it under my bomber jacket. When operatives from the French Resistance came to get me out of there and back to freedom, I could take it with me. It was worthless to Jean. He had let the grime build up over it. He wouldn't even miss it.

Back in Canada, it could eventually turn me into a millionaire. I would hang on to it for a while and then sell it in the United States. To make myself feel better, I reasoned that I could send money to the Noels after the war, lots of money, more and more as the years went by, to make up for what I had done. They wouldn't be surprised, since it would be to thank them for saving my life. I told myself that they didn't need a million dollars, that it would spoil them, that a hundred thousand or so would make their lives very comfortable, just perfect. And so, I rationalized my sin away.

But the devil's plans don't always work out.

I had assumed—in fact the Noels and the local Maquis (that's what the French Resistance people were known as in France) had assumed—that getting me out of the Arles area would be part of a well-orchestrated plan. In fact, the day that everything happened, three Maquis men were at the house, putting that plan in place.

It was not unusual for farmers to sell or share a wagonload of hay with a neighbor, so the Maquis came that day, dressed in their peasant clothes, and worked in the field at first, getting a full load of hay onto a wooden wagon. Then they spirited me out of the barn and we all sat around the kitchen table, plotting my escape. But in the middle of things, a truckload of Milice came roaring up the road toward the farmhouse. The road approached from the far side of the barn, and so I was trapped. If I had rushed back to my grave in the barn, the Milice would have seen me. But in seconds they would be inside the house.

I saw flashes of fear cross over my comrades' faces, matching the terror inside me. But they were brave and able and used to functioning well in moments of great danger, and instantly hit upon a solution to our situation. With Yvette holding her hand over her mouth so she wouldn't scream, I was bundled out the back door of the house at just the right moment, toward the nearby wagonload of hay. The house momentarily blocked the Milice's view of us and in seconds I was shoved under the mountain of hay. With a calm, lazy crack of the whip, the three Maquis drove the wagon slowly away, moving us back down the road, waving goodbye to our hosts after a hard day's work in the field. Miraculously, the Milice didn't suspect us. We didn't stop until we reached Spain—the Maquis couldn't risk unloading me anywhere. Everything happened very fast. I never again saw the Noels or that Van Gogh painting.

You are probably wondering what I want you to do. It is a task that I am reluctant to ask of you but one I dearly hope you can achieve.

I have spent many nights over the past sixty-five-plus years thinking about that painting, and what I did or was planning to do. I could never bring myself to tell the Noels about the fortune I found in their barn. I sent them money after the war, but I was too ashamed to do anything more. If I told them my secret, they would know I had wanted to deceive them, that I had wanted to keep the money for myself. But now, after my death, the truth can be told, not just to you, but to them.

Please, Adam, go to France and find them or find where their children or grandchildren live and tell them what I never had the courage to tell them myself. Their little farm is likely long gone now, along with the painting. They lived in the countryside, ten miles or so northwest of Arles, halfway to Nîmes. The closest place was a village called Bellegarde.

I know this is a very difficult assignment, and not just because the family will probably be hard to find after *all these years. But if you can do this for me, I know I will rest much easier...forever.*

And then you can go on to try the next task.

We weren't far from the border. The US officials always asked you lots of questions when you crossed over—everyone was a suspected terrorist these days. I was wondering if I would even be able to speak if they grilled me. But inside, I had no doubts. The contents of the letter had thrilled me. I knew I would do everything I could to accomplish this first task. I *had* to. I *had* to be the one who restored my grandfather's honor.

FIVE
VANESSA ENCHANTED

I could hardly wait for school to be over for the year so we could go to France. The only thing that made it bearable was Vanessa Lincoln. I remember that first day back at school, after I'd received my task, as if it were yesterday. It started out the way it always did: I took the long way to my locker, making sure I passed by hers. I'm sure many guys did that. I moved quickly so Shirley wouldn't catch up to me. I don't think she knows why I take that particular route each morning, though sometimes I wonder if she does. Girls seem to know a lot of things.

And there was Vanessa, wearing those tight jeans (as usual) and a form-fitting sweater (she seemed to have a boatload of them). Her blond hair was doing that blowing-in-the-wind thing in the dead air of the hallway, and she was ignoring everyone except her few close girlfriends and that guy who looked like that tennis star, Rafael Nadal, and played in the school's coolest alt band. I hated his guts. His locker was only about five away from hers. She seemed to adore him and he barely talked to her. There was something wrong with him.

Anyway, I walked by and she didn't even notice me. But then, something occurred to me.

"Vanessa," I said.

No response.

"Vanessa, my grandfather is sending me to France."

She looked up. Those blue eyes were the color of the sky on a perfect summer day.

"I thought he died. It's so sad."

"Yeah, well, he was ninety-two."

"And a war hero."

"That's, uh, kind of why he's sending me to France."

She looked around, as if she were gauging whether or not she wanted to be seen talking to me for this long.

"What do you mean?"

I can tell a pretty mean story when I want to. Must be something I inherited from Grandpa. It's the only thing I do well around girls. I laid the basic idea out for her, told her many of the things I wasn't even supposed to tell my parents. But I had to. It was the only truly effective ammunition I had with her.

I could see her falling for it as I moved into the more dramatic stuff, so I gave it everything I had. I shaped things so that Grandpa didn't look so bad, because if I killed off his reputation in the process then this just wouldn't work. I said that he had intended to sell the painting for the Noel family and give them all the money, but that he had failed on all counts because of the Nazis. I was charged with the romantic mission of making things right. By the end, those beautiful blue eyes were looking kind of moist.

"That's amazing," she said quietly. She was actually glowing. The Nadal look-alike walked by, and she didn't even turn her head. I could have sworn that he was a little annoyed. "If you accomplished this,

Adam (she'd never called me by my first name before), that would be so…heroic."

Bingo.

✦

Over the following days, I kept up the pressure, toying with the emotions of one Vanessa Lincoln, babe of my dreams. I purposely hadn't told her about the other two tasks. That's because the key to telling a dramatic story is the pacing. You can't give your listeners all the candy right off the bat. You have to dole it out bit by bit, making the payoff even better and better, until you get them to the story's climax.

I couldn't, of course, tell her exactly what the other tasks were because I didn't know myself, but I came up with all sorts of World War II intrigue involving spies and dangerous endeavors, speculating that I might have to put myself in real danger, perhaps bring to justice people who did terrible things during the Holocaust, perhaps right some significant international wrongs. I made it seem like there might be some women in danger.

I got her, hook, line and sinker. I kept reminding her of my schedule as time went by, sort of putting her on a countdown during the days before I was to leave on my mission. She was pretty intrigued by the way Grandpa had set things up, the idea of having to accomplish one task before going on to the other. She was dying to know what was in the last letter. "That sounds just like him!" she said.

Shirley found out that I was talking to the Big V a lot more than I used to—I think girls have spy networks—and she wasn't very pleased. Not that she said much. Shirley isn't like that. But I wasn't getting as many kisses as before and they weren't delivered with nearly as much feeling. I was getting the message, and it bothered me. Like I said, I really like Shirley. Actually, she's pretty awesome. She's in good shape, and she's on the school basketball and volleyball teams even though she isn't that big, and she has these really kind dark eyes and short dark hair that I've heard the other girls tell her is "cute." Her last name is Sandoval—she has some Spanish in her, which makes her seem kind of exotic. And she's a great person too. Rarely gives me a hard time and gets even better marks than me in school.

She helps me with a guy named Leon Worth who has a degenerative muscle disease and is in a wheelchair. He stopped growing a while ago and is awfully small. His muscles are just fading away. It's pretty sad, so last year I volunteered to help him out whenever I could by getting him from class to class and making sure he has his meals. I find myself thinking about him a lot, wishing he had a better life. Shirley says she started liking me when she saw me spending so much time with Leon. Now, she probably helps him even more than I do. My parents just love her.

But we are talking about Vanessa Lincoln here. And I wasn't actually doing anything with her anyway. I wasn't even touching her. I certainly didn't make any commitments—until that last day.

❊

We had booked our flight for France for the week after school ended, so my last day at McKinley High was a pretty big deal. I'd let all my buddies know what I was doing (though I didn't tell them as much as I told Vanessa, and I told *her* that I didn't tell them as much, which was a smart move, tactically). So I was a pretty popular guy that last day. I'm not proud of the fact that I found a way to elude Shirley for just the right amount of time after the last bell rang, so I could have some V-time. I eluded Leon too. I wasn't proud of that either, most definitely, but I couldn't be with him and Ms. Lincoln at the same time. Vanessa had actually asked me to come and talk to her that day.

While we chatted, I looked around to make sure Shirley was nowhere in sight. Vanessa talked about my trip to France. She was touching me too, doing that thing that girls do when they like you—"accidentally" putting one of their soft hands on your arm. We exchanged (get this!) our home and email addresses and our cell numbers. I couldn't believe it! She asked me to write to her when I was in France, and gave me her details on a little sheet of pink paper, in that looping, flowery handwriting all girls have. And then she drew a happy face at the bottom (like I've heard she always does when she signs something) and a heart! Then she kissed me.

Well, it wasn't like a *kiss* kiss on the lips. It wasn't remotely like the kind I was looking forward to getting from Miss Sandoval the night before I left, but it was a genuine kiss, right on the cheek and

pretty close to the lips. She did it real fast and unex-
pectedly, and I almost fell over.

"Write to me, Adam, write to me lots. I want to
know *everything*! And when you come home, when
you've done all those tasks, we should…maybe…
start seeing more of each other."

Shirley came around the corner at that moment.
She had Leon with her. I don't think she saw the
kiss, and there wasn't any evidence of it on my cheek
since the Big V wasn't wearing lipstick that day. She
goes for a "natural look." I've heard other girls say
that about her in kind of bitter voices. It means she
looks like she's got no makeup on when, I guess, she
really does. But she sure smelled good up close, kept
her eyes open, looking at me when she kissed me, and
left a little bit of something on my cheek, something
see-through and a bit sticky. I think girls call it gloss…
lip gloss? I rubbed it off and jammed the piece of pink
paper into my pocket before Shirley reached me.

✤

We were kind of quiet on our walk home that day. She
took my hand but didn't squeeze it like she often does.

I kept worrying about what she'd seen. We live in a pretty nice part of Buffalo called Delaware Park, not far from our school. It has museums and parks and is full of beautiful houses. Most people think my city is a bit of an armpit, but that's just because it's cold and snowy in the winter (and that's only because it's so close to Canada). Our area has lots of trees and boulevards and trendy restaurants. Mom and Dad say they wouldn't live anywhere else. She can make some big sales here and he can get from our "leafy street" to the airport in fifteen minutes.

But the neighborhood didn't feel comforting to me as we walked along the street that day. There was a bit of a frost coming from my girlfriend, and it was hard to blame her. Even though she didn't see the kiss (at least, I don't think she did), she somehow, without saying a single word (strange how girls can do that), made it crystal clear that she was bummed out about my spending some of my last minutes at school with the best-looking girl in the place. Her hand was limp in mine. I didn't know how to respond. Guys never do. It seems like girls spend all their time, from the moment they are young and playing with Barbie dolls, figuring out relationships, learning how to react to certain situations. Guys don't do anything like that. We don't have any practice whatsoever. So when there is a romantic crisis, when the shit hits the fan, we don't have a clue. We are always just running on autopilot.

But I still think I did a pretty good job of making things up to her over the next few days. I bought her a teddy bear. Girls like them from guys. She wasn't much for showing emotion, but she started to cry when I gave it to her. That kind of shocked me, since she wasn't like most girls that way. When she started crying, I moved in for a hug, which seemed to work just fine. She hugged me back like we weren't ever going to see each other again. It felt awfully good. I let my guard down and really hugged her back.

"You know I like you for who you really are, Adam," she said quietly.

"What does that mean?"

"Like right now, when you aren't trying to impress anyone. It's just you and me, and no bull."

I knew there was some criticism mixed in there, but it went along with a pretty tight snuggle from a really great girl. All my worries melted away for a moment.

That was how we parted. I spent the rest of the evening reading over Grandpa's letter. Then I turned to the other two and that small white one. What if I just opened them all up now? He'd never know. I was dying to know what was in them. The first task was pretty hard and involved all sorts of cool secrets. I couldn't even imagine how interesting the other two might be. But I held myself back. Something told me that I'd ruin everything if I cheated. I just stared at the outside of the other letters. The two big manila ones were thick, obviously containing long letters just like the first. Then I glanced at the last one. That was the letter I *really* wanted to open. What in the world was in it? Was it the secret to my grandfather's entire life? Was it something even bigger than that? Something he'd discovered long ago and had told no one? I couldn't resist holding it up to the light. But I couldn't see anything.

I was going to do everything in my power to open that last little white envelope before I returned from France.

***

Before we left the next day, I made sure I had Vanessa's info. I looked at the piece of paper for a while, following the beautiful, flowery, feminine lettering.

I smelled it, like I had about fifty times already. I put on the clothes I was going to wear on the plane and made sure her note was in my wallet in my pocket. I wanted it safe, even though I'd also put her information into my cell phone.

At the last moment, I gave Leon a call.

"Hello, Mr. Murphy," his squeaky voice said over the phone. "You have reached me on my distant planet." He likes to say that whenever I call him. He often slurs his words too, and a lot of people can't understand him. But I can. And he always refers to me as "Mr. Murphy." I think he's making fun of me.

"I, uh, I'll miss you, buddy."

"No, you won't."

He has this terrible way of always knowing the truth or at least most it. I was going to miss him, but I probably wouldn't be thinking about him too much. I imagined his face on the other end of the line, his smile, his bright blond hair.

"And forget about Vanessa Lincoln," he added. I thought I'd hidden my interest from him. "Leave her to me. Shirley's your girl. She's the best. And you know it."

He also had a way of making me think about what I was doing. It took me a little while to get my mind back on the trip. But when I did, I realized something that for some freaking reason I hadn't thought about for even a moment during my heady days with Vanessa Lincoln. My heart began to pound and I felt sick to my stomach.

You actually have to fly on an airplane to get to France!

SIX

IN THE AIR

I had the barf bag on my lap all the way. The actual flights—Buffalo to New York, then New York to Paris—took about nine or ten hours all told, and my face was as white as one of Vanessa's form-fitting sweaters every inch of the journey. I kept thinking about how high in the air we were, how ridiculous it was to be 50,000 feet up in the sky, or whatever it was. *In the air*, for God's sake, with nothing holding you up! And down below, at least most of the way, was the Atlantic Ocean. An *ocean* for Pete's sake, about a million miles across and about a million feet deep!

Most kids could show their fear in a situation like that, but not me. Not the grandson of the great World War II aviator and son of the decorated Gulf War fighter pilot and genuine hero. We were on an overnight flight, but I didn't sleep very much. When the sun came up I was just sitting there, pretending I was enjoying a movie, gripping the arms on the seat like I was going to rip them out. The only thing that got me through the flight was the thought of my mission in France.

When we finally reached Paris, I wanted to get down and kiss the floor of the Charles de Gaulle Airport. But we weren't in Paris for long. My parents had asked me whether I wanted to do the "Paris thing" at the beginning of the trip or at the end, and I opted for the end. I was anxious to get going. It wouldn't be possible for me to appreciate the Eiffel Tower or the art galleries that Mom would want me to see, with that first task waiting for me in southern France.

We traveled European-style and took trains to Marseille. First, we got on these red, white and blue subway cars (I don't know how the French get away with using America's colors) in the airport so we could get to the Gare du Nord (that means the Northern

Railway Station) in downtown Paris. That station was very old and pretty cool, built about a thousand years ago (like everything in Europe) and made out of stone. It looked like a palace on the outside and had massive skylights with crisscrossing steel beams.

My choice would have been to take the TGV or *Train à Grand Vitesse* (that means "very fast train") from there to Marseille. I saw one on a track, sleek and ready to roll, said to be able to travel at nearly 200 miles per hour and capable of getting us to our destination, nearly 800 kilometers away (for some reason, the French, just like Canadians, use kilometers instead of miles), in about three hours. But Mom wanted to travel on the horse-and-buggy train, which would take us nearly twice as long. She said I should "see France, not rip through it." Ripping through it would have suited me just fine.

But the train ride turned out okay. As we rumbled along, I couldn't believe how small everything was, even in Paris, where there weren't any real skyscrapers that I could see, other than the Eiffel Tower. I actually didn't spend too much time working any games on my phone, which is unusual for me. I stared out the train window most of the way to Provence.

(That's the "region" that Marseille is in. Kind of like a state, I guess.) Everything outside the city looked small and old too: the houses, the narrow roads, the cars. And they kept looking older as we moved south, like we were going back in time. Things in America were twice the size and twice as new. I hadn't heard of most of the places we passed through, though the countryside, I must admit, was nice to look at, full of green rolling fields, stone walls, blue rivers and lots of flowers. Mom called it "delightful." The French themselves were a colorful lot too. The women (who looked awfully good to me) were slim and wore all the colors of the rainbow, and the men dressed a little on the feminine side for my liking.

But Marseille wasn't so delightful. First off, I couldn't believe how big it was, especially for a place I'd never even heard of before Grandpa mentioned it. It was probably even bigger than Buffalo. Secondly, it wasn't the cleanest or richest place, especially around the Gare de Saint-Charles (the train station), and it felt kind of dangerous there too. It wasn't entirely uninteresting though. It seemed kind of Arab and African in places, kind of mysterious. Marseille got a lot better when we took a cab through the city and ended up down near the water. The Mediterranean Sea, as blue as can be, is spectacular, and Mom and Dad had booked a really nice hotel, right near the water. It was kind of artsy inside, filled with weird sculptures and paintings that hung on walls that were scrubbed to look rough and old. By the time we got there, it was dark and we were all exhausted. Even though it wasn't much past nine o'clock local time, we were still on American time and we all just collapsed into the two beds.

My parents, especially Mom, were reluctant to let me go the next morning. We'd all slept about twelve hours and Mom tried to convince me to stay with them for another day or two to become adjusted to the time change. But I wanted to get moving. I was anxious from the moment I got up.

They bundled me into a cab. Mom told the Arab driver to take me to Arles and gave him the name of the hotel she had booked for me there. Dad clapped me on the shoulder and wished me good luck, his rock jaw firmly set, while Mom gave me a hug and a kiss, and kept the tears back. She's actually really good at that for a Mom. Still, she made me promise to text her every day.

And then I was off. Sixteen years old and alone in southern France, armed with some money (though Euros looked like Monopoly money to me) and a prepaid bank card with a $2,000 limit. I was ready for my mission.

✦

It was about forty miles to Arles, and the cabdriver, who said nothing other than "*Américain*?" five seconds after we took off, drove about a million miles an hour to our destination, as if he couldn't get there fast enough. That suited me just fine, though the trip was a little hairy in places, since he didn't seem to pay a lot of attention to the road, humming away to Arabic music that blared out of his earphones.

On the way, I realized that I hadn't let Shirley know that I was across the ocean and safe and sound. I texted her four words: In France am OK. Then I dropped a few words to Leon. Then I thought of Vanessa. I should let her know too. But when I started to text I realized that I had a lot more to say to her, so I switched to email and really went at it. I must have written five hundred words before I realized it.

I made the start to my adventure seem heroic, even though I hadn't really done anything yet.

Arles was very different from Marseille. It was much smaller, really just a big town, with a historical and, I have to say, kind of magical atmosphere to it. The houses were yellow or light blue or red and jammed along narrow streets that wound around the beautiful Rhone River. It was what Mom would call picturesque. There was even a big Roman amphitheater, a real one from back in the day, in the midst of things. People moved at a slow pace; there were lots of tourists. Sitting at cafés drinking coffee or simply taking in the sights seemed to be the order of the day. Hardly anyone appeared to be working, except those who were serving at the hotels, restaurants and stores, and they certainly didn't seem to be laboring too hard. They were much friendlier here than in Marseille.

My downtown hotel was very old and painted yellow, which I thought was perfect, since Van Gogh was so into that color. Before I left Buffalo, I had gotten a book out of the library about him and a lot of it had dealt with his time in Arles. I could certainly imagine him living in this town, in his rustic old "yellow house" with another great artist named Paul Gauguin.

Van Gogh struggled to get by, hardly eating anything, painting all day (and I mean *all* day) in the country-side, drinking at night with working-class folks in the cafés, spending time with loose women in "houses of ill repute," fighting with Gauguin…and cutting off his own ear. No one's really sure why. Throughout it all, he kept painting masterpieces (though no one back then thought of them in that way). He was a pretty crazy guy, but there was something about him that was truly cool, beyond the great paintings he did. He was a genius and he didn't care about being rich or famous. He just believed in his art. It all came from his heart. I like that. No one thinks like that anymore.

It was exciting to be alone in a hotel, especially in southern France, but I didn't spend much time thinking about it. Mom had bought me a sandwich and a drink to consume on the way to Arles, so I didn't need to eat right away. I checked in, settled into my small room with its old bed and desk and yellow stucco walls, and immediately started studying my map. Grandpa had said that the Noels' little farm was about halfway between Arles and a place called Nîmes, not far from the village of Bellegarde. I found Marseille, then Arles and then Nîmes on the map. I found a road that looked like a pretty major one, running between those two places. And right there, right between them, was Bellegarde! My heart began to race. It looked like there was lots of countryside in the area. I imagined my grandfather being there long ago and felt as if I was about to walk around in a place from a story.

While I was looking at the map, I caught a glimpse of myself in the mirror. I stood up and checked out my look. Though I wished I could grow decent stubble, I was very tall for my age and really not so horrible-looking. My eyes were almost black and my hair was dark and I liked to keep it uncombed, so it had that rumpled look that I'd heard girls like. Shirley seemed to anyway. She liked just about everything about me. But I wondered, too, as I gazed at myself: was I capable of doing what my grandfather was asking of me? And what if I couldn't? What would I tell Vanessa? What if I couldn't even do the first task? That would be devastating.

I paced in the room for the rest of the afternoon, imagining what might happen tomorrow, and what, exactly, I should do. The Noels would be really old now, their two children about seventy. Maybe none of them were still alive, not even the children;

maybe there would be no trace of them at all. Perhaps no one around here would remember them. Would this be a wild-goose chase? Was it ridiculous?

I went out and ate in the café next to the hotel, getting by on my fractured French, helped out by a good-looking young waitress, probably about seventeen or eighteen. She had short ragged blond hair, cut to look like it had been torn, and a big smile. She was wearing a long white T-shirt with the word *L'Amour* written on it, over black-and-yellow-striped tights. She had a bright orange scarf wrapped around her neck, looking like she had just tossed it there, and yet it was perfect. And very artistic. She asked "*Américain?*" before I even opened my mouth, and then giggled and pointed out what she thought I might eat. I wondered how she knew where I was from. I was wearing jeans (good ones, mind you, bought in an outlet mall in Buffalo) and my best Aéropostale T-shirt. I knew that was a French word, something to do with air, so I thought it made sense to wear it here. In fact, I had two of them and intended to wear them both a lot on this trip.

I went for a walk after I finished eating and tried to imagine what it must have been like for Van Gogh in the 1880s. Because the town was so historical—other than the cars and people in modern clothing, it didn't look like it had changed a great deal—it was easy to believe I was seeing what he saw. I strolled north along the river to the place where his yellow house once stood and found a plaque with a reproduction of one of his paintings on it, but little else. Just a park and some busy streets. It didn't matter; his art lived on. I went back to the hotel and got into bed early. Despite the time change and how exhausted I was, it was hard to sleep. I was too excited. I couldn't wait for tomorrow. I knew that it would change my life.

SEVEN
REVELATION IN THE COUNTRYSIDE

I got the concierge (I couldn't believe how they pronounced that in France, so weird) at the hotel, who spoke fairly good English, to hail a taxi for me and let the driver know that I wanted to go to the village of Bellegarde, and that I was looking for someone named Jean Noel in that area. My driver wasn't an Arab man this time, but a French woman, middle-aged and chain-smoking but as slim as a straw and dressed as colorfully and stylishly as my waitress had been. She talked all the way to Bellegarde, which thankfully was only about fifteen minutes away. She kept waving her arms as she spoke, popping her

cigarette in and out of her mouth. I didn't
stand a word she said.

I told her my plan was to start at the City Hall or
a tourism booth, but she did me a favor by paying
no attention and insisting that I get out in front of a
café that looked like the most popular place in town.
I immediately had the feeling that you could find
anyone in this neck of the woods if you asked at this
establishment. It was packed, even at this early hour,
and they were all obviously locals—no fancy Paris or
even Marseille styling was going on. They were plainly
dressed, or at least as plainly dressed as the French
could be, which wasn't all that plain and a lot fancier
than most Americans. Many were sitting outside.
The windows, which ran the length of the building,
were wide open, so you could see everyone inside too.

I strode past the outdoor customers, who were
leaning over their little round metal tables,
drinking coffee and wine (believe it or not, at this
hour), eating bread and cheese or quiche or crepes,
everyone talking loudly, waving their hands to
make what appeared to be very important points.
I walked up to the counter inside, half expecting
someone to ask me to leave, since this was obviously

...denced by the wine. But no one

...egan, very slowly and loudly,
...d that the louder and slower I spoke
...d be to understand my American
English, ... for...someone...named...Jean Noel."

The man behind the counter introduced himself as Monsieur Leblanc, the owner, and said something very quickly. It may or may not have been "Jean Noel?" It sounded like "Sha-nole?"

I plucked up my courage.

"*Et sa femme Yvette!*" My French teacher would be very proud.

"Yvette!" cried someone nearby. "*Jean et Yvette Noel?*" There was no doubt about what *he* had said. I turned toward the outdoor seating area to see an old man rising to his feet, the legs of his ornate metal chair grinding on the stones. He wore a blue beret and a long double-breasted coat, even though it was a warm summer day. Once he was standing, he struggled toward me, using his cane to keep upright.

"*Américain?*" he asked as he approached.

"*Oui.*"

"*Pourquoi cherchez-vous les Noels?*" He had a big veiny nose and bloodshot blue eyes. He smiled at me with a look of genuine kindness. But he had spoken so fast that I had absolutely no idea what he had said. I turned to the café owner, who surprised me by saying, "He wants to know why it is that you search for *la famille Noel.*" It was pretty heavily accented English, but certainly understandable, thank goodness.

I spoke slowly. "Tell him…that my grandfather… was an American pilot…shot down…near here… during the Second World War. The Noels…found him…and kept him…in their home…safe from the Nazis…and the Milice."

The old man had looked toward the café owner partway through my speech, searching for the correct translation, but his head snapped back at me when he heard the word *Milice.*

The owner translated what I had said and as he did, the old man began staring at me, absolutely staring, as if he had seen a ghost, and then his eyes filled with tears. He looked at me for the longest time, then seized me by the face, kissed me on both cheeks and then on the lips. It was absolutely disgusting.

He turned to the entire café and shouted what sounded like, "*C'est le petit-fils de David McLean! C'est le petit-fils de David McLean!!!*" Even I knew that "*petit-fils*" meant grandson. There were maybe thirty customers seated at the tables. Half of them—the younger ones—remained exactly as they were, still talking or staring at their newspapers. Another quarter looked up with interest—they were middle-aged. And the last quarter—the elderly—immediately struggled to their feet and began to shout and cheer in my direction. Within moments, they were coming toward me as fast as they could go (which wasn't very fast—it was like a mob of elderly groupies coming at me in slow motion) and soon they were surrounding me, each and every one trying to lay another peck on my cheek.

❉

Fifteen minutes later, I was in Monsieur Leblanc's little Citroën car, the old man in the front passenger seat and me stuffed into the back, knees up near my chin. Every now and then, the old man would turn around and grip my hand and pat it.

They were taking me to the Noels' home.

I couldn't believe it. It would have been pretty cool if that home were simply where the descendants—the children and their children—lived now, in Bellegarde or Arles, but no, as Monsieur Leblanc made clear in his translations, we were actually heading to the little farmhouse where my grandfather had been harbored nearly seventy years ago!

My heart was pounding as I listened to him.

"The home is still standing," Monsieur Leblanc said.

"It is?"

"*Mais oui*, but Monsieur et Madame Noel do not live there anymore."

"They are alive?"

"Of course. We peasants live long, hardy lives *en Provence*." He didn't pronounce his *h*s. I wondered why he couldn't just spit them out. It wasn't *that* hard.

"That's amazing."

"Not as amazing as your being here is to the older people of Bellegarde. I am sure that word is spreading through the village. Apparently your grandfather, Monsieur McLean, was a—how do you say?—a celebrity around here. He was the only American pilot the Resistance found near here and got to safety.

We all know that your grandfather was very kind to the Noels after that, sent them money that made their lives bearable, allowing them to move to a nice house near Bellegarde, since a few years ago."

"Just a few years ago?"

"They are very stubborn people. Their children—their daughter Lise is retired *en Paris* and their son Antoine was a, uh, air-traffic controller at the *aéroport en Marseille* and is retired there too—they could not convince the old people to leave their home until recently. It had no indoor plumbing, no electric heat, nothing, but they would not move. But now, they must. For *le démolition*, you know."

"Demolition?"

"They are building many new homes here, what you Americans call, I believe, a subdivision. Rich people, they like to live in southern France, you know. It is fashionable in these parts—the home of Van Gogh *et* Gauguin—and it has gorgeous weather."

I had noticed how many new homes were in the region. The roads were busy and the countryside was receding. It looked like very little farming was going on anymore.

"Nothing has been done to their home yet. There were protests, you know, and *le démolition* was held up by the courts. But it is set now. It will happen before the end of the summer. They will be paid nicely for their home."

The old man in the front seat shouted and gesticulated wildly with his hands.

"*Oui*, Paul." Leblanc turned to me. "He says that does not matter, that they should leave the Noels home alone, that it should be a monument, that all of La France is going to, uh, hell. Or is in the shithouse, as he actually said."

"The subdivisions kind of remind me of Buffalo," I said.

Paul blurted something else out.

"But he also says they all wondered why your grandfather never came back. He would have been welcomed as a hero."

I paused. "Yes, uh, I don't know. I never asked him."

"*Voilà!*" cried Paul.

"*Oui*. Here it is!" said Monsieur Leblanc.

We had turned off the highway onto a narrow road lined with old fences and were approaching two small stone buildings. They were even smaller than I imagined. I remembered Grandpa saying in his letter that on the fateful day the Milice had come to the Noel home, they had approached from a direction that made it impossible for him to be rushed to the barn from the house without being seen. It was clear now that he was right. The two buildings were about twenty feet apart and I could see the gap between them. If I'd had a gun, I could have picked off anyone running from one to the other. The stone buildings were ancient—tiny, with old orange-tiled roofs—and they looked as if they were about to fall down. Old wagons and barrels were strewn about on long, uncut grass.

We pulled up to the front door and I got out. It was the first time in my life that I had ever been speechless. Here was the setting for that amazing story my grandfather had told me, a drama about espionage, life-and-death moments of bravery...and betrayal. To me, it was a setting from a fairy tale come to life.

I walked forward and touched the outside walls, thinking that Grandpa had touched them long ago.

"The Noels are coming," said Monsieur Leblanc, taking his cell phone from his ear. "Someone is bringing them."

I glanced at the barn.

"They are very, very excited!"

I thought of what I had to do. My stomach began to churn. How was I going to tell them?

"*Entrez-vous!*" said Monsieur Leblanc, taking me by the hand and ushering me toward the front door the way someone might motion to a king. But I didn't feel like royalty at that moment. I felt like the grandson of a jerk. It was a strange feeling. I had never felt that way about him before. But my idol now had feet of clay.

The house was so small that it almost made me cry. It felt damp inside. There was the meager stone fireplace, cold ashes left behind, an open doorway leading to the tiny bedroom, not much bigger than a closet. There was a musty smell. I pulled out a wooden chair at the wooden table and sat down with a thump.

"*Oui*, it must be overwhelming for you," said Monsieur Leblanc.

"I-I'd like to see the barn before the Noels get here. That was where they kept him. It might be too much for me to see it with them."

"*Bien sur*," said Paul, taking me by the hand and leading me back through the entrance. Once outdoors,

I let him take the lead. He was a little hard of hearing and as we walked, Monsieur Leblanc whispered into my ear.

"Paul was a Maquis, a member of the Resistance. The older folk around here think very much of him. He told me in the car that he knew the men who got your grandfather out. He thinks of them as heroes and he—what is the word?—reveres Monsieur McLean too."

The barn was even smaller than the house. My head almost touched the ceiling. It was hard to believe that one or two animals could be kept here, let alone the horse, cows, pigs and chickens of so long ago. But it was evident the minute we entered that all residents were long gone. The smell of old manure was in the air, but the building was silent and filled with cobwebs.

Just as Grandpa had said, there was the small stall with feed bins for cows, a smaller one behind with troughs for pigs and, past it, against the far wall, an even smaller area where the chickens had been kept. I left my hosts and stepped over the low board fence into the pigpen and approached the coop. There was no evidence of a grave-sized disturbance in the soil, but I could see that it would have fit perfectly against the wall and been well separated from the pigs, an unattractive place for the Milice to want to search. It was very clever.

Tears nearly came to my eyes *again*, and I'm not a crier, not remotely. But I imagined my young grandfather lying here nearly seventy years ago, frightened out of his mind, buried in the soil, breathing through a straw, praying that he might live another day, evil all around him.

Then I looked up on the wall and saw it. Nailed to a beam and barely visible behind a blanket of thick cobwebs and covered in grime was a *painting*! I could tell that its dominant color was yellow. It was a miracle.

I heard the sound of a vehicle rumbling up the road. It stopped outside the house, much the way the Milice had roared to a halt near the very same spot long ago, looking for an American to kill.

"*Allo! ALLO!!!*"

The Noels had arrived.

EIGHT

MY MOMENT COMES

They were the sweetest people on earth. I had never met such gentle, decent folks. Mr. Noel still looked big and powerful. Dressed in a long blue coat, under which I could see a shirt and tie, he struggled up from the little car and stared at me as I left the barn, his face glowing. I stood there looking back (probably the spitting image of my grandfather). But he didn't come toward me. Instead, he turned and put his big hand back into the car and, like the gentleman he was, helped his wife, his bride of more than seventy years, from her seat. Though unsure on his own feet, he gallantly steadied her, putting his arm around her waist and guiding her toward me, allowing her to greet me first. Yvette was at least a foot shorter than him and wearing a thick coat far too hot for today but obviously her Sunday best. It was only unbuttoned at the collar. She wore a flower-patterned dress underneath and black shoes with thick heels, the latter not helping her ability to stay upright. Her face was round and open, her glasses circular, her white hair just wisps now under her fancy hat with its bright feather. I could see that it had once been a pretty face. Still was, actually.

"*Monsieur Murphy?*" she asked as they shuffled as fast as they could toward me.

"*Oui,*" I said softly.

"*Le petit-fils de David McLean?*"

"*Oui.*"

"*Oh!*" she gasped and almost fell into my arms. A second later, Jean had enveloped me too, both of them gripping me in a family hug.

�֍

I couldn't do it.

There were many opportunities that morning. We sat at the wooden table in the house talking for more than an hour, Yvette holding my hand the entire time, staring into my face as if I were a miracle. They knew Grandpa had died. His will had left them a series of payments to be made until their deaths, and even some money for their family afterward. They asked many questions about him: how he had been over the last few years, what his wife had been like, his children, his grandchildren. They said how thankful they were for all he had given them and remarked on how he had been suddenly taken from them; how they hadn't seen him since the moment the Resistance spirited him away in the hay wagon that summer day in 1944. They wanted to know why I had come alone. That took a great deal of explaining. I said that I had been a sort of favorite of my grandfather and that he was an eccentric sort (they laughed when that was translated) and that he had, for some reason, asked in his will that I come alone and that I do exactly as I was told (they laughed at that too). I said that my parents were in Marseille and I had to keep in touch with them and get back there soon.

And of course, they too asked why he had never come back to see them. I could see tears well up in their eyes. But they insisted they understood. David McLean was an important man, a busy man, a family man.

"Not that busy," I said quietly. When that was translated, Yvette took my face in her hands and kissed me.

But that was the closest I came to an apology, at least at the house. They invited me to their home near Bellegarde for a meal and wouldn't take no for an answer. So I was bundled back into Monsieur Leblanc's little Citroën and brought to their apartment halfway between their old farm and the village center. Paul was still with us, more than happy to tag along for a meal. I was pleased to see that their place, on the bottom floor of a new complex in one of the new subdivisions, was modern and well furnished, and that their granddaughter, also named Yvette, was looking after them.

"*Votre grand-père payait pour tout cela!*" cried Jean as he proudly showed me around.

"That means, your grandfather paid for all of this, including young Yvette's wage," said Monsieur Leblanc.

While that was nice to hear, it didn't make up for his staying silent. He had given them thousands when they should have had millions. All throughout dinner—chicken pie and fresh salad followed by sweet pastry from a local bakery—served on their best china, I had a hard time concentrating on the conversation, and not just because it was being translated.

I had to do it. I had to apologize.

I thought of what it might do, of the silence that would ensue, the nearly lifelong bubble it would burst. My grandfather's reputation would be shattered. But this was what he wanted. He wanted it all made right. I also thought of his words in his letter. He had warned me that it would be difficult. But in all my excitement about coming here, of accomplishing his tasks and finally proving myself to him, even from beyond the grave, I hadn't thought enough about just *how* difficult it would be. It was, as he had said, almost impossible.

But I really wanted to achieve it. And I really wanted to move on to the next task. Did I have the courage to do as he asked? I thought about Vanessa and what she would think of me if I accomplished nothing on my mission.

I looked at the two old smiling faces glowing at me.

❖

Three hours later I left their home, after kissing them both on the cheeks (which was definitely the first time I'd ever done anything like that!) and receiving their hugs and taking in Yvette's heartfelt tears. All without revealing my grandfather's secret.

I felt like a failure.

But as Monsieur Leblanc drove me back to Arles that night I wondered if I had really failed. Would I have felt even remotely like I'd been successful if I had told those two wonderful old people the truth? That, at least, was what I told myself.

When I reached the hotel I sat on the bed for a long time, just looking out my little window over Arles, home of Vincent Van Gogh. I kept rationalizing what I had done (or not done, really), and after an hour or so, with the sun beginning to set, I started to convince myself that I had completed the first task.

"There is no way," I said out loud, "had he been there with me in their home today, that he would have wanted me to tell them." I told myself that several times. Then I pulled the big manila envelopes and the little white one out of my suitcase and set them on the bed beside me.

I really, *really* wanted to open the next one.

I had gone there. I had spoken to the Noels. I had actually been in the little house and the barn. I had even seen the painting. I had done all that I could. He would have wanted me to go on to the next task.

Then I started thinking about the painting. *It was still there.* The building was about to be demolished.

In another hour I had made a decision. I got into bed and lay there, wide awake, throughout the night.

❖

In the morning, I asked the concierge to hail me another cab and told the driver to take me to Bellegarde. But when I was halfway there, far out into the country-side, and could see the slight elevation in the distance where the little farmhouse was, I asked to be let out. The driver gave me a strange look. We were still on a busy highway. But he pulled over and out I got.

It was a hot day in southern France, and I must have walked several miles along the side of that highway. I had chosen to wear my jacket, despite the heat—it was part of my plan. When I came to the little side road that led to the farmhouse, I paused. But then I kept moving, right up to the overgrown yard and into the barn.

Though it was silent inside, I could hear the sounds of the long-dead animals that had lived there, of the Nazi planes buzzing overheard, of the Milice racing their vehicle to this house, trying to find my grandfather. And when I listened very carefully, I could hear him breathing through his straw, terrified.

I could also feel his excitement when he saw that painting, and feel the pain in his heart when he made his decision. I stepped toward it. I could, at least, take it into my hands, brush back the grime and look at it.

I wiped the cobwebs away, gently pulled the crude homemade frame off the barn boards and took it into my hands. As I brushed more grime away, the yellow, the reds, the blues, began to glow. It was absolutely stunning. How could anyone ever have thought that this masterpiece was junk? It was so beautiful.

It was also nearly invaluable. During the years since my grandfather had been here, Van Gogh's paintings had become almost priceless. His work was now among the world's most valuable—only Picasso's art rivaled it. I had done some investigating online after I read Grandpa's letter. I looked down at the word *VINCENT* now evident on the striking baby-blue vase in his picture.

How many *millions* of dollars was I holding in my hands?

I was completely alone. No one knew about this. No one knew I had it. *No one.*

I unzipped my jacket, put the painting inside, zipped it back up and walked out the door.

The guilt overwhelmed me as I trudged down the road toward the highway, but it didn't stop me. I began making my argument, out loud.

"This is an impossible situation. I *cannot* tell them, but it is ridiculous to leave the painting there. It will be destroyed during the demolition. That wouldn't be right. Would it really make sense to break their hearts or do a great disservice to art, to history?"

No.

I sped up and was now sort of marching.

"I will keep it, somehow, and not tell anyone. Then ten years from now, I will make up a story about how I got it. Perhaps I purchased it in a flea market or found it...yes, *found* it in a Dumpster or something.

Or I could make another trip to France and say I found it then. And when I sell it, I will give a great deal of what I make to the Noels' children, to their grand-children, whose lives will be changed. And I could still keep millions. I could buy Vanessa anything."

I reached the highway. Little French cars buzzed past me. It was a long walk back to Arles. I tucked the painting farther down into my jacket and began to move at a brisker pace, almost running.

"This is the only solution, the best solution. Everyone will benefit."

A loud sound came toward me from behind and I nearly jumped out of my skin. I recognized it. I wasn't sure why. Probably because I had heard exactly that same thing in movies set in France. It was the sound of a French police car. They don't wail like our sirens, high-pitched and frightening. They are frightening in a different way, blaring one short note then one long, over and over again.

I turned around and saw the police car. My heart raced. Then I realized that it couldn't be coming after me. Then, I was sure that it was!

I started to run. Not a good move. The cruiser (though that's a generous word, since French police cars are about the size of American riding mowers) kept coming after me, pulling over to the narrow shoulder and zipping right up behind me. Finally I stopped, foolishly clutching at the painting inside my jacket. How did they know? Were they watching the farmhouse?

"*Bonjour*," said the cop who got out of the car. "*Américain?*" I thought he looked angry.

"*Oui*," I said, my voice cracking, as I pulled out my passport and handed it over. That's what Mom and Dad had said to do if I ever got into trouble.

"Why are you running?" he asked, examining it with a frown. I was glad that he at least spoke English.

"No—no reason."

"No reason?" He looked me up and down. I was certain that he paused at my midsection, where I clutched the painting close to my chest. I wondered if the wise thing was to simply hand it over.

"Do you realize how serious your crime is?"

"I...I..." I had totally lost the ability to speak.

"Not," he said with a smile, "all that serious." He handed the passport back.

"Huh?"

"You must not walk along the side of a freeway in *la France, mon ami.* Get in. I shall take you to your residence."

"You—"

"Tell me: are you a fan of Kobe Bryant?"

"Kobe?"

"Yes, a fine sportsman. I like. But, you know, I do not think he could ride a bicycle well, which is the most difficult of all the athletics. Lance Armstrong: now there is *un Américain sensationnel!*"

He clapped his hand on my shoulder and ushered me into the back of the cruiser, where I sat hunched over, the painting digging into my gut, listening to him and his partner as they went on about American sports heroes. My heart never stopped pounding. In less than ten minutes, they had dropped me at the hotel.

"Monsieur Américain, stay away from such bad crimes while you are here," the cop said with a grin as they roared off. "Keep your nose washed!"

I slinked up the stairs to my room, sure that everyone in the hotel knew what I had under my jacket. Once inside my door, I hid the painting at the bottom of my suitcase, under all my clothes. Then I started to pace, back and forth, back and forth, the wooden floor creaking as I moved. I told myself that I had no choice now. I had the painting and I couldn't risk taking it back. Someone might catch me and then *all*—my whole life—would be lost. I would rot in a French jail, guilty of robbery. And I would deserve it. What I had just done was typical of me. My hands were shaking. I had done something incredibly stupid and wrong, and now I had to live with it. I imagined someone coming up here and finding the painting. What, in God's name, had I done?

But after a while, I started to calm down. I used all the arguments I'd employed while walking away from the farmhouse. I could make this into a positive thing for everyone. I had to believe that. The painting was small and it would sail through airport security in my suitcase. Or would it?

I sat down and took a deep breath.

I tried to stay positive. And soon I was thinking about Vanessa again. I could make all this sound awfully good to her. I took out my cell and started emailing her. But then I stopped. What if I wrote her a letter, an old-fashioned letter? She'd find that awfully romantic. There was lots of stationery in the room, fancy stuff with the hotel's name on it, looking very artistic, with lots of yellow. Very Van Gogh, very French. She would think that was really cool.

It was hard going. The last time I'd written a letter was for a pen-pal thing when I was a little kid. But I worked hard, tried to find the right words, the ones I imagined a girl would like to hear, and got it done, making sure it was several pages long. I told her that I had found the Noels and the painting and that I was about to reveal its value to them. I made it sound pretty dramatic. I'd figure out a way to tell her the truth later on. I sealed it and wrote her address on the outside of the envelope in my best handwriting. I would ask the concierge for a stamp later.

I knew I should write to Shirley too. I could almost hear Leon's squeaky voice telling me that she was the best girl for me. I'd only sent her that one quick text when I arrived. I should ask her how Leon was making out too. I was sure she would be checking on him, and that made me feel good.

But I never wrote her that email, because when I reached for my cell, I happened to glance down at the open suitcase. Sitting on top of my clothes, dug up from the bottom where they once had been hidden, were the other two manila envelopes and the small white one.

That was when it occurred to me that in all my excitement I hadn't even given another thought to the fact that, in essence, I had reached the next level in my assignments. It really seemed to me that no reasonable person could have expected me to have done any more with my first task. Could they?

I picked up the second envelope and opened it.

NINE
THE SECOND ENVELOPE

Dear Adam,

Congratulations. You did it! I want to thank you from the bottom of my heart. You are a better man than me.

I almost stopped reading at that point. I set the letter down, feeling terrible guilt. But soon those arguments rose inside me again, telling me that I had done what I could and that there was no turning back. So I read on.

As I've already mentioned, this second task, believe it or not, is even more difficult than the first. I wouldn't blame you if you simply read what I have to say here and then joined your Mom and Dad for a nice vacation before heading home. You have done enough.

But if you choose to go on, here is your next challenge.

During the war, Corsica had seventeen American airbases on it. In fact, they used to call it the "USS Corsica." But not all of us who flew reconnaissance missions from that Mediterranean island were from overseas. French fliers, who had bravely fought the Nazis for as long as possible, had formed a Free French Air Force and many were stationed near us.

The problem was, the Americans didn't like them very much. The Yanks had their way of doing things and, more importantly, they resented that many French had collapsed at the beginning of the war and worked with the Nazis. The Americans didn't respect their flying abilities either. So the two sides kept their distance and sometimes were even hostile to each other.

But not me. Maybe it was because I was Canadian, I don't know. But I thank God today that I wasn't bitter toward them because my attitude allowed me to befriend the most extraordinary man I ever met. He is at the heart of your second task.

You will recall that I often read to you from a novel entitled The Little Prince when you were a child. It was always my favorite, and your cousins may have mentioned that I read it to them too. You probably forget the story now, but it is one of the greatest ever written, the tale of a pilot who crashes in a desert and meets a strange little person who appears out of nowhere and changes his life. *Le Petit Prince*, as it's known in French, is one of the bestselling novels of all time; the Harry Potter books took a long time to catch up. But there is something that I never told you about that novel. I wanted to keep it a secret, which fits the book's air of mystery. I knew the incredible man who wrote it.

I met him in Corsica. His name was Antoine de Saint-Exupéry, or as his friends knew him, "St. Ex." He was a legend in France, even before he wrote the book. You wouldn't have thought that if you'd met him. He was a big man, very tall and a bit chubby, who walked with a lazy, loping gait and had a little turned-up Mickey Mouse nose and sleepy black eyes with lids that seemed always about to close.

But he had a giant spirit and a giant heart. He was an adventurer, a hero, a matchless storyteller, with a charisma that women, children and even the odd grown man, like me, could not resist. I feel deeply honored to have even spoken with him.

He was one of France's earliest aviators, taking to the air in the days when that meant taking your life into your hands.

99

And when the French decided that they wanted to fly mail from Europe to Africa and South America, across deserts and oceans and jungles, only the greatest swashbuckling fliers were used. He was one of them. That first airmail service made its pilots into national heroes, who flew by sight and often crashed in desolate places. Everyone in France was astonished at their feats. The very name of their company— Aéropostale—became a symbol of courage and adventure.

"Aéropostale?" I looked down at my shirt. "So that's what that's all about."

The great "St. Ex" was their biggest star. He would land his plane anywhere, in any conditions, to find and rescue his comrades. But he was different from the rest. He not only accomplished these feats, he could retell them too. Speaking in desert tents or Parisian restaurants, he could rivet audiences, his magnetic presence lighting up his surroundings.

Then he began writing, his stories set in the skies. Within a few years he was one of France's greatest authors.

But he couldn't stop flying, and the danger increased. As he headed toward his forties, many of his fellow pilots had been killed. His own accidents, some particularly gruesome and spectacular, began to take their toll on his body and mind.

And then the war came. He immediately volunteered to fight and was in the first plane to spot the Nazi panzer divisions thundering toward Paris in the evil blitz that started World War II. When he described it in print, it was poetry.

After Hitler overran a divided France, Saint-Exupéry was devastated. A romantic who was angered by the brutality of war, he was fed up with the bloodthirstiness on all sides. He wanted to side with humanity. He fled to New York City. He was soon criticized as a traitor who was staying out of the battle.

And so he came back, to fight the Nazis the only way he knew how.

But he was well past his prime, battered and bruised by his horrific accidents and ill-equipped to fly new-fangled planes with complex instruments. His friends feared that he was giving his life away for France and freedom.

He soon found his way to Corsica.

But while living in the United States, he'd written The Little Prince, a children's story often read by adults, about imagination, friendship and the human spirit, about what was possible in a time of hatred. It appeared in print just as he landed in the Mediterranean, just as I came there too.

I soon heard stories about him from French pilots, tales that were by turns thrilling, sad and hilarious. The great man had been grounded more than once by the powerful American air command. They couldn't believe that his request to report had even been allowed. He was ten years too old, broken, so large that he had to be shoe-horned into cockpits, almost incapable of operating the smoking-fast Lockheed P-38 Lightning planes that were the pride of the US Air Force. Americans guarded these expensive flying weapons as if they were gold, and "Major X" (as they called him) often crashed them. He seemed to the Yanks like someone from outer space: he would forget to wear his oxygen mask at 30,000 feet, write while flying, read while flying, take photographs of parts of France he loved instead of what he was supposed to be spying on, knew little English so he couldn't understand the men in the control towers (Americans who didn't know a word of French) and often let his wheels down only seconds before landing, bringing ambulances hurtling to the airstrips. He once circled the airfield for nearly an hour after a dangerous mission while he finished reading a gripping mystery novel.

But the French loved him. He gave them hope and courage, a walking monument who could describe life and what was truly important in it like no one had done before.

I knew him for a short while, a precious while. In the summer of 1944, just before I left on the mission that ended in my being shot down over Arles, I was stationed in Bastia in the northern part of the island, close to where he was. I had just read The Little Prince almost fresh off the press. Not one of my American colleagues even knew it existed.

But I loved it. I even loved the ending, when the Little Prince, this amazing miniature man from another planet, dies. It was so sad that I had to stick my head under the covers in my cot and cry.

I desperately wanted to meet St. Ex, so I got permission to take a jeep the six miles from our base to the beautiful village of Erbalunga, where his famous squadron was living. I was greeted with surprise. Americans never visited the French, unless they were commanders telling them what to do (despite the fact that the French pilots were often more experienced than the Americans). When I arrived, St. Ex was holding court outdoors after a picnic breakfast that looked and smelled delicious. He was telling a story and the others were listening with rapt attention, their mouths actually hanging open. He noticed me approaching and though I think he knew I couldn't understand a word he was saying, put a finger to his lips and motioned for me to sit down and listen. He held me spellbound too. I felt I was in the sky with him, soaring with him, crashing with him. When he was done, there was silence. Then he stood up, produced a deck of cards from his sleeve and went through a series of tricks that had us all in stitches. But I noticed that he had scars around his eyes and one that snaked up from his mouth, and I could tell that it was hard for him to stand.

Every day that week in early June, I went back to visit him. He was enchanted by my interest and signed my book. We talked and talked, me in English, he in French, laughing and hugging each other, two citizens of the world communicating with our souls.

I became so enthralled with him that I decided to give him a gift. I liked to carve in those days and found a remarkable glowing pink rock on the beach. I'm not even sure what kind of rock it was. But it was a pretty good size and I carved into it one of his beautiful passages about friendship from The Little Prince, using a little stone chisel and a club hammer from back at the base. When I gave it to him, he was moved to tears and told me that he would keep it with him on every flight he made. He said this as if it were an important promise.

The very next day, I went on my fateful mission over enemy territory and lost touch with St. Ex for more than a month. But when I was rescued, I was taken back to Corsica from Spain for a short while for debriefing. And as soon as I could, I went to see him. I was shocked by his appearance. He seemed to have aged terribly. His body was finished with the world, though his spirit remained. He greeted me with a smile.

The next day I saw him go up on a mission. I had the sense that he was sneaking up, had not been properly cleared to fly. His friends had to tie his shoes for him and help him into the plane. He reached down before he took off and waved to me, holding my rock aloft.

When he was in the air, a French pilot who spoke English remarked to me, "St. Ex has come here to die."

And so he did.

The following week, on July 31, he took off at about 8:30 AM to photograph and map enemy-occupied land in southern France. Some say he had been grounded the day before but went into the skies regardless.

He never came back.

There were many myths about what happened to him. More than one German claimed to have shot the legend down. But no trace of him was found. It was as if he had vanished, age 44, in 1944. In the single saddest day of the Little Prince's life, there had been 44 sunsets on his tiny planet.

St. Ex had returned to his home in the skies.

I remember my extreme sadness. I remember the anger I felt too, when I heard an American pilot report, about midafternoon, after St. Ex had been gone for too many hours, that a "Frenchie," who was apparently a writer, had not returned. I wanted to bust him right in the chops.

Within weeks the Allies landed on the southern coast of France and began to squeeze the Nazis from the north and south.

When I got back to North America, I kept waiting to hear news that St. Ex had been found. But Paris fell to us, and then we marched into Germany, found the horrific extermination camps, the coward Hitler killed himself and finally his villains surrendered, but St. Ex never reappeared.

Then, more than half a century later, in 1998, a miracle happened. A fisherman working off the coast of Marseille found a rusted old 1940s bracelet in his net. It bore the name of Antoine de Saint-Exupéry. After a few years of underwater searches, the wreckage of his Lockheed P-38 Lightning was discovered on the floor of the Mediterranean Sea nearby, 250 feet deep. The plane's fuselage, propellers, landing gear bay and all sorts of other bits and pieces formed a line of debris nearly half a mile long.

His plane had dropped straight down into the water.

Did he decide to leave the earth? Was he hit by enemy fire? No one will ever know. And that seems fitting.

But there is something else that I would like to know, that I need to know.

That fatal day, was St. Ex carrying the gift I gave him? Did my extraordinary friend actually take the mark of our friendship with him to his death?

That is your task, Adam. I will say no more.

TEN
SEARCHING THE DEEPS

I sat and stared at the last page for almost a minute. How, in the name of one of Vanessa Lincoln's sweaters, was I going to do this? The letter gave me so few clues. Grandpa wasn't kidding when he said this was beyond difficult. The wreckage had been found more than a decade ago, off the coast of Marseille. Almost every trace of it was gone now and it had been 250 feet deep anyway!

I had only tried underwater diving once, during a holiday Mom and Dad and I went on in the Caribbean two years ago. It had been pretty simple stuff: just puttering around using a snorkel in shallow water as clear as blue glass, looking at exotic fish. We were planning to go again next year and swim with dolphins.

Two hundred and fifty feet deep? That seemed like an awfully long way down. And when I got down there, I'd be looking for a needle in a haystack or, more accurately, a rock in a sea, which was even worse.

But I wasn't going to give up. The odds had been stacked against me in the first task, and I'd achieved it, hadn't I? Sort of? I got to my feet and started to pace. Soon I'd made up my mind that there was no use trying to be clever about this. There was only one way I would have any chance of accomplishing the task. It was straightforward. I had to discover exactly where the wreckage had been and then find a way to the bottom of the Mediterranean. Which one first? I wondered if there was some way to kill two birds with one stone. Local divers likely knew all about this famous wreck.

I grabbed the Provençal phone book, which I assumed had Marseille listings in it. What was the French word for diving? I thought of my private lessons and recalled a related word, the one for swimming pool, because it was so rude. *Piscine*, pronounced something like "pees-in," or as I preferred to say, "piss-in." I remembered having a good laugh at that and telling my friends—all of whom I'm sure had peed in pools at one time or another—about it. For once, being crude was turning out to be helpful. I was sure I could connect the word for pool to the one for diving. *Jean dives into the pool.* How would you say that? I was certain I had learned it. And then it came to me: *Jean plongées dans la piscine. Plongée* or something very close to it meant *dive*! I flipped through the phone book.

There it was: *Plongée Sous-Marine.* Underwater diving. There were about ten businesses offering scuba-diving instruction to beginners and expeditions for advanced divers. I picked one called Plongée Internationale, whose advertisement was partly in English.

I didn't want to call them on my cell since I was afraid that I would have a difficult time understanding them. There was a much better chance of us communicating clearly in person, especially considering that I had such a complicated request.

It was just a little past noon. I got a stamp at the front desk, mailed my letter to Vanessa and headed down to the restaurant where the young waitress worked.

She was wearing a very short dress today, loose and plain and white, almost see-through, her only decoration a red scarf. But she looked great, of course, seemingly unconcerned about her revealing apparel. She had changed her hair. It was spiked today. She gave me that knowing smile, suggested a different meal and took her time bringing it to me. There was something about her style that made me envious. She didn't seem anxious about life, the way I was, the way all my friends were back in Buffalo. She seemed to be moving slowly and happily through life, satisfied to be doing what she was doing. I knew there was a word for her. Finally, it came to me. *Natural.*

The concierge hailed me another cab, and by two o'clock I was headed toward Marseille, a little concerned about ending up somewhere in the city not far from where Mom and Dad were staying. Though I'd been texting them every day, saying I was okay, I didn't want them to see me or know what I was doing. This was between Grandpa and me.

But I need not have worried. The cabdriver never even entered Marseille. He got on a highway just to the north and drove around the city, dropping me in a suburban area to the south. It was a pretty laid-back neighborhood. There were a few homes and businesses and a sandy beach. The coastline was rocky and led to a point in the Mediterranean. When I got out and stood facing the blue sea, I could see Marseille to my right with its big buildings and docks and rocky islands off its shore. To my left, a few miles in the distance, were more rugged islands and a huge expanse of water, seemingly endless, with almost no horizon. St. Ex had gone down somewhere way out there. Somehow, I was supposed to find a little rock he *might* have had?

Plongée Internationale was at the far end of a street not more than a two-minute walk from the water, and it was indeed set up for tourists. It was two stories high and fairly large, its stucco exterior painted blue like the sea, with fake palm trees outside and a sign that read *We Speak English* over the door with an American flag beside it. The building smelled of rubber and seaweed. There wasn't much to the interior, at least as far as I could see. The first room was small, with a counter and shelves piled high with all sorts of rubber suits and scuba-diving equipment. There were photos on the walls of amazing under-water scenes in crystal-clear blue water and a video of similar adventures played on a screen in the corner of the room. There was a staircase leading upstairs, and I could see a big room through a wide doorway behind the counter. Obviously this outer area was simply for sign up. All the action took place elsewhere.

There was just one man behind the counter. His face was bronzed from the sun and his long hair was reddish and tinged with a gray that streaked through his ponytail and was more prominent on the beard that grew uncontrolled across his face. He was in shorts and a T-shirt bearing the company logo, and his flip-flops snapped on the floor whenever he moved. He looked up when I entered and gave me a smile that was obviously forced. His whole life must have been spent dealing with tourists. I was glad I was tall, since I hoped he'd think I was a little older than sixteen.

"*Américain?*" he asked.

I wished they'd stop doing that.

"*Oui.*"

"What can I do for you, my friend?" I didn't have the sense that he was my friend. But he knew I could pay. I'm sure he was thinking, Young American, out on his own.

I explained what I was after and watched as he smirked.

"What you are asking, my friend, it is impossible."

"Why?"

"Why? Because, unless you are an internationally acclaimed diver—and I know many of them and they are mostly French—then this cannot be done. Nitrogen narcosis—rapture of the deep—have you heard of that? The bends?"

I considered lying. "No," I finally said.

"I thought not. Let us just say that that sort of depth is…out of your depth, and most everyone else's too. *C'est impossible!* Most tourists we take to maybe fifty feet, maximum. There are regulations too. No one, certainly no tourist, is allowed to go as deep as you want to go." He looked down at his books again.

"But I need to see that site!"

He raised his head again, as if my comment was a great intrusion on his time and dignity.

"Then you will need an atmospheric diving suit, you know, with a helmet and full body covering."

"How much?" I took out the bank card my grandfather had given me. The man looked down at it. A sort of greedy expression passed over his face, then disappeared.

"No. Americans, they think they can buy anything."

"No?"

"You are an amateur, my friend. You said so yourself, before you began with your fantasy story about Saint-Exupéry and his plane. You admitted that you were not experienced at all. I will *not* put you in a suit!" This time he glared at me.

"But I must—"

"There is nothing to see there! It is all gone, just like him. What are you looking for anyway? He wasn't carrying gold, you know. He wasn't that sort of man. What mattered to him was, you know, inside here." He pointed to his chest.

"I'm not looking for gold. I can't say what it is."

"And I cannot help you." He looked down at his books again and didn't look up.

I began to walk away, back to the door. This was a disheartening dead-end. I was guessing that all the other diving places would have similar rules. If I couldn't go down there myself—and that seemed absolutely impossible—I certainly couldn't trust anyone else with the task of looking for my grandfather's rock. Maybe I should buy a diving suit from a different supplier, without revealing that I was about to use it, and try this alone? Or pay someone to take me underwater illegally? I stopped at the door.

"Do not consider trying this, in any way," added the pony-tailed man, who had obviously seen me pause. "If you do it, you will die."

Well, that ended that possibility. I absolutely couldn't dive by myself. Was there *anything* else I could do to make this happen? At least this guy had spoken to me again. Maybe I could get something out of him about the crash site, the wreckage. Maybe he could lead me to the people who found the plane.

"You," I said, turning around, "you said that there was nothing to see at the site. How do you know that?"

"I have been there." He wasn't even looking up.

"You what?"

"Of course!" He looked up and smiled at me. "We all have. This is St. Ex, my friend! This was the greatest find in our lifetime."

"Where is it?"

He paused. "I suppose there is no harm in telling you. If you stand outside my shop and look to your left, around the point there, you will see a series of islands, an…archipelago, no? *L'île de Riou*, a place of rocks."

"Yes."

"St. Ex went straight down out there that day, some kilometers in that direction over the water, maybe four kilometers from the shore?"

"Really? That is the actual spot?"

"But his body, it has never been found. They will never find it! And we will never know what happened that night. It is a mystery, no? St. Ex, he was a mysterious man. He knew things we do not know. He knew the truth. He has gone back to his planet!"

"I don't want to find his bones or any—"

"Then, what *do* you want?"

I said nothing.

He smiled. "You, young man, are an unusual *Américain*. They never ask about someone like Antoine de Saint-Exupéry. They ask only about the nightclubs, the wine, the women or the men. But you—you want to be near the great soul of *la France*. That is unique; that is admirable."

I could tell he was leading up to something.

"I know a man here who helped with the St. Ex dives. He is an artist of the waves. He will be impressed with you. He might help you. He has a…what is the word? A submersible?"

"A summer saw blue?" That was honestly what I thought he'd said. And that comment almost lost it for me. He wasn't pleased with my imitation of his accent. But I couldn't help it. I didn't know what he meant.

"*Un sous-marin.* A submarine," he said tersely.

"A submarine?"

"A little one. *Un petit.* A man and a boy could fit in it. I will make a contact to him for you."

✦

The next day I received a call on my cell from the man at the diving place. He had talked to his friend, who he described first as an oceanographer then as a marine scientist and then as a "guy who likes to invent things," and told him about my interest in St. Ex. The friend had apparently been impressed. He was planning to make a few dives in his submersible that week and was willing to let me go with him.

I was thrilled out of my mind.

But I wasn't nearly as thrilled when I met my submarine captain. He was standing on the rocks a few miles east of Plongée Internationale, exactly where I was told he would be, the top of his wet suit stripped

off and his hairy, naked back turned to me as he stared
out over the sea. He was gazing in the direction of l'île
de Riou. It was a gorgeous day, the water deep blue and
lapping gently on the shore, the sky a lighter blue and
cloudless, the white and gray rocks rising up like sculptures on the islands a few miles away. The sea smelled
of fish and algae. The submersible was anchored just
offshore, a miniature submarine that looked like the
one on the cover of one of Dad's Beatles' records from
eons ago. It really did. It was even yellow and painted
with brightly colored peace signs. It was so small that
it looked like a toy. I wondered how the two of us
would even get into it. It was patched in places too,
which didn't inspire much confidence. A thick hose lay
on the rocks in huge coils, tethering the submersible
to what appeared to be a massive oil tank or oxygen
chamber. It looked like there were literally miles of
that hose. A big truck was parked nearby on the little
rocky road. A boy of about thirteen or so stood beside
the tank and turned to look at me when I approached,
though he never said a word. He was wearing designer
jeans that were so low-riding that I could see most of
his underwear and the top of the crack of his butt.
Not a pretty sight. He wore a torn T-shirt with the

words *Le Punk* on it, and his dark hair was done up in some version of dreadlocks. He completely ignored me as I walked by him and right up to the pilot, who I assumed was his father.

"Monsieur Halliday?"

The man nearly jumped out of his wet suit and into the sea.

"*Mon dieu!*" he cried. "You-you terrify me!" He put his hand over his heart. Or at least I think that was where it was. The gray hair on his chest was so thick that it was hard to tell. A bear would have been proud of such a coat. But he wasn't built like a bruin. He was as skinny as a rail and the hair on his head was at least as impressive—or unimpressive—as his chest hair. It hung down almost to his nipples and looked like it hadn't been combed in decades, although he immediately began tying it up in a knot, as if suddenly ready for action.

He seemed to instantly forget that I'd scared him. He beamed at me. "*Américain, oui?*"

"*Oui.*"

"But you, monsieur, are not like all the rest?"

"I—"

"You want to find *le location du poet du ciel, oui?* You want to be near him?"

"The poet of the sky? Saint-Exupéry? *Oui*."

"Ah!" He stood for a long time and just smiled broadly at me. I felt very uncomfortable. Then he took me into his arms and hugged me and wouldn't let go. It was hard to know what to do. His behavior seemed very inappropriate. And yet somehow I feared nothing from this guy. For one thing, he was about half a foot shorter than me. His arms and legs were like matchsticks. I could snap him in half, if need be.

"Peace," I heard him say quietly.

But suddenly he came out of the hug and was all action, making frantic motions, crying out to the boy ("Johnny!") to let some of the hose loose and turn on various things, to bring my wet suit to me so I could get into it and offering instructions that I could barely understand, three-quarters French and one-quarter English.

But as soon as I was wedged tightly behind him in the submersible, and we were underwater, I forgot all his weird ways. Our surroundings were stunningly beautiful and crystal clear, like being inside *Finding Nemo*, on the world's largest 3-D screen, 360 degrees around and many feet deep. Awesome, brightly colored fish swam by. Some stopped to gawk at us.

Sea plants waved in the water. I was absolutely blown away. Leon would have fit in this little sub with us easily. He'd love this. But this was the sort of thing he'd never get to do. We plunged lower and lower, and I could feel pressure in my chest. Then we started to move farther out to sea.

Monsieur Halliday was very kind to me that day. When we got to the area that was obviously the crash site—obvious only because he said "*Voilà!*" and turned a light on and began flashing it around on the sea floor—he spent a great deal of time there. We moved back and forth over that half-mile area many, many times.

"*Le tombe du St. Ex!*" he cried out more than once as tears rolled down his cheeks. It was indeed moving, though I wasn't about to cry.

But unfortunately what was most moving about it was a sense of absence, the sense that all traces of the great man and his plane were gone. The divers and oceanographers had picked the sea floor clean. And rocks? There were acres of them, most covered with algae and barnacles. They all looked the same.

I stared like an eagle at every rock that came into sight, hoping to see one that could be Grandpa's, but it was obvious that I was *literally* looking for something even more elusive than a needle in a haystack. Floating among all of that beauty, privileged and lucky to be there, in the very spot where the creator of *The Little Prince* died—and deeply moved by it—I could feel my heart sink, lower than the very depths we were in. I finally let Halliday take us back up to shore.

All the way home, he went on and on, half in French and half in English, about how impressed he was at my interest in St. Ex, how moved he was to have shown it to me, how remarkable it was that I didn't seem to want to leave the site and had insisted on seeing every inch of the floor with the searchlight.

We got out and stripped off our suits, young Johnny still not saying a single word. Mr. Halliday was reluctant to take the stack of Euros I offered him but, in the end, accepted them and hugged me tightly again, tears in his eyes, and kissed me four times on each cheek. I was about to say goodbye, when he mentioned something that stopped me cold.

"I wish, monsieur, that you could have…*plongé avec nous*…uh, dived with us on that important day. I had…*mes mains*…my hands on the pieces of the plane itself. I was just a…assistant…*mais*…I touch the things St. Ex touch. I even give Johnny here a—how do I say it?—gift…from the plane."

"A gift?"

"We could not, you know, keep anything from the plane itself, *mais*…I found a rock in the cockpit."

"A rock?"

"*Oui.* I turned it over, and underneath it was, uh, remarkable. It was *un couleur un peu bizarre*—"

"Bizarre? It was…it was a strange color?" My heart began to pound.

"*Oui.* It must have smashed through the cockpit window of the plane when it crashed. So it was not part of the plane but it had been inside it. I thought that was special, especially *le couleur bizarre*, so I give it to Johnny."

My head snapped over to butt-crack boy. I must have given him a strange look, because he actually stepped away from me. What if this rock hadn't smashed through the cockpit window from the outside when the plane struck the bottom of the sea? What if it was already in the cockpit, carried there by Antoine de Saint-Exupéry?

"Did it say anything?" I asked.

Halliday looked a little alarmed. "Say anything? *Dit quelque chose?* Monsieur, it was a rock."

"Was there anything written on it?"

He appeared relieved. "*Mon ami,*" he chuckled, "what a strange thing to say! It came in through the window! It had many algae *sur le surface*, no? And barnacles? Johnny was two year old, maybe three, but I just thought he would like *le couleur, et—*"

"I want to see it. Now!"

ELEVEN
MESSAGE FROM THE SEA

I had to wait for them to pack up the submersible, and it just about drove me nuts. It must have taken an hour. I wanted to scream.

While I paced around, I wrote a long email to Vanessa. I told her all about being under the Mediterranean Sea, the beauty down there, the romance of seeking St. Ex's crash site and the building excitement of this assignment. Then I texted Shirley, but by then the submersible was almost on the truck. Going well, was all I had time to say.

We made our way to the Halliday's home out on a nearby point, at the end of a dirt road far away from everyone else but with a nearly 360-degree view of the water. Just the two of them lived there. There wasn't any sign of a female resident, believe me. It was a ramshackle wooden place that looked as if Mr. Halliday had whacked it together with a hammer and nails. It was probably worth about one-tenth of his submersible. The living quarters were tiny and cluttered with dirty clothing and dirty dishes and filled with a horrible smell I couldn't identify. I counted five dogs and nine cats, and they seemed to have the run of the place. Attached to the house at the back was a lab of some sort, about three or four times the size of the living area. I could see microscopes and sea plants and fish skeletons on lab tables; a lovely odor was emanating from there too. I kept my distance.

"Johnny!" cried Halliday. "Show Monsieur Murphy le rock." But Johnny was slouching along with his earbuds in, listening to a thrash metal band that was growling out French lyrics like the lead singer was Satan's PR guy. It was so loud that I could almost make out every word. (*Les Américains* and *diable* came out clear as a bell.) Halliday had to rip the buds from his ears and repeat himself. Johnny didn't look pleased.

The boy reluctantly led me to his little room, not much bigger than a walk-in closet and even more cluttered than the living area. I wasn't even sure where his bed was at first, because it was under mounds of clothes and toys and video games and other electronic equipment. Other than the posters on the walls (of a bunch of hard-core bands I'd never heard of), the only items that weren't mixed into this rubble was a laptop that formed the peak of the mountain on his bed and a large flat-screen TV on a shelf. It was blaring when we came in.

He began rummaging around in the piles. And as he worked, he actually said something, the very first words he'd uttered since I'd met him, spitting it out under his breath in a sort of snarl. "*Américain,*" he hissed. Then he muttered, "*Capitaliste!*" It was a pretty strange thing for a kid his age to say.

Finally, he found what he was looking for. I could tell because he suddenly stopped moving and stood up. His back was to me. I stiffened. Then my hands started to tingle.

When he turned, he was holding a rock a little larger than a man's fist. It was mostly covered in barnacles and algae, but part of one side, probably the side on which it had rested in the cockpit, was an unusual pink and purple color; it actually glowed.

I reached for it.

But he pulled it back.

"Money," he said. He pronounced the word with barely the trace of an accent. He rubbed the thumb of his left hand against his index finger and smiled. It wasn't a pleasant grin.

I took out a few Euros and handed them to him. He snorted but snatched them. I reached out again, but again he pulled the rock back.

"Just to look," he said.

"You've got to be kidding me, butt-head," I snapped, then instantly prayed that he didn't understand.

He gave me a funny look but did not hand over the rock. "Money," he said again.

I gave him a few more Euros and ripped the rock from his hands.

"Hey!" he cried.

I pulled it away, thrilled to have it in my grasp, wondering if this indeed was the rock my grandfather had carved and given to the one-and-only Antoine de Saint-Exupéry!

There wasn't a single word carved onto the glowing part, not that I could see. And the rest was just a mass of hardened green growth. At first, I felt like throwing it through the kid's window. But then I had an idea. I marched out of the room—butt-crack boy in pursuit, cursing me in French—and headed for the lab. Mr. Halliday put himself between his kid and me, and that allowed me to slip into the lab, find a screwdriver, sit down and get to work.

My hosts were soon looking on, the father standing slightly in front of the son to keep him from interfering.

I started on the side of the rock that needed the least amount of work, the side that was partially clear. The rest of this bottom part was only covered in algae—no barnacles. I scrubbed it clean with a cloth. What appeared was more of the glowing surface of the rock, shining purple and pink. But there were no words carved into it either. With a sigh, I turned the whole rock over. Maybe this thing was just what Halliday thought it was: a big unusual stone that had smashed through the window of the cockpit when the plane crashed to the ocean floor. Maybe it had zero connection to St. Ex and Grandpa.

I began grinding the thick wall of barnacles off this side. I worked until I had chipped a hole in that wall. Then I actually gasped. I saw something carved into the rock at the bottom of the hole I had created. I began working frantically. Soon a little word emerged... *friend.*

I held the rock up to my face, my hands shaking so much that I dropped it with a thud, almost cracking the lab table.

Halliday picked it up and stared down into the opening I had scraped in the barnacles. "*Mon dieu!*" he cried. Scurrying away, he found an electric tool of some sort—it was hard to tell exactly what it was—and began buzzing the rest of the barnacles off the rock. Once he'd sheared them almost to the surface, the two of us picked up screwdrivers again and carefully chipped off the last bits. Le Punk stood beside us, still peeved.

Another tiny word emerged and then another. Soon there were fifteen.

I have made him my friend and now he is unique in all the world.

I stood there with that rock in my hands, my mouth wide open, just staring at it. Halliday was moved too.

He put his hand on my shoulder. Though he likely knew it was a sentence from *The Little Prince*, he had no idea what it meant to me. All the same, he was stunned. It was as if this item had appeared by magic, out of the ocean and into the plane of the soul of France. He looked at me as if I were a messenger from God.

I turned to the boy, emptied my pockets of Euros, which he took with glee, and walked out the door, still almost in a trance.

"Monsieur!" cried Halliday at the door. "Where are you going?"

"I have a letter to read," I said.

That made little sense to him, of course, but he nodded. A messenger from God can do and say what he wants.

TWELVE
THE THIRD ENVELOPE

The minute I got back to my hotel, I put the rock in the suitcase with the painting and opened the third envelope. It wasn't as thick as the other two. This is what it said:

Dear Adam,

Wow! You have reached the third level! If I am in any way conscious right now and aware of what is going on down (or up!) on earth, I am certain that I am dancing in the air.

I wouldn't be so sure about that, Grandpa.

You are ready for the most difficult task of all. Read this and make your choice. Do not feel compelled to try it. In fact, I am reluctant to ask you. There is danger involved.

Here it is.

The Noels were not, as I mentioned in the first letter, a literate family. But like so many people (or peoples) who do not write, they loved to tell stories, believed in legends and had many superstitions. I remember Yvette throwing a pinch of salt over her shoulder at every meal because she was certain it would help her and her husband live long lives. And when they had had a great deal of wine, their stories would become more and more fantastic. During the month I was with them, they told me tales—using gestures, drawings and what little French I could grasp—of ghosts and giants who, they claimed, used to roam southern France long ago; and of lions and rhinoceroses that, in their imaginations, were the French beasts of bygone days.

They also liked to talk about caves. I understood from them that many other people in the region did as well. The area they lived in, and more exactly the land to the north and northwest, was very hilly and rocky, actually mountainous in places, and prehistoric passages ran into and through these elevations. Jean's stories often started in such caves and told of ferocious men with superhuman powers emerging from them to do extraordinary things. Those men, he said, had the power to create wonderful art. They were, Provençal folklore insists, the world's first artists. They drew fabulous depictions of themselves and of animals on the walls inside their mountains. Jean's yarns sometimes started from that artwork—stories of incredible beings stepping out from the stone and coming to life.

He said that several ancient caves with drawings had been found in the past half century. But he was fond of predicting that THE cave, the GREAT cave, had yet to be discovered. In it, the world would see history's oldest art—and when modern people viewed it, they would be astonished. This work, he often said, would be magical. It would show the world the meaning of life. He insisted that this was not a dream—one day such a place would actually be uncovered. The discoverer would be a local person, because they can almost "smell" the caves.

I, of course, took what Jean said on these subjects with a pinch of salt even more substantial than what Yvette used to fling over her shoulder. In other words, I didn't believe him.

But when I returned home, I decided to read a little about French caves and learned that much of what he had been trying to tell me was true. In the early twentieth century, several remarkable caves had been located in France, all with ancient drawings on their walls. Perhaps the greatest was the Lascaux Cave, stumbled upon in 1940, just four years before I ended up with the Noels. It was situated just a few hours northwest of Arles. But no respected writer, no scholar, ever said anything about the great cave that contains "the meaning of life."

Until 1994.

I distinctly remember the day I picked up a copy of the New York Times and read of the groundbreaking discovery of a new cave in southern France that had the worldwide science community stunned. It had been found by three local people, one named Chauvet, who had been walking along the side of some cliffs in a semi-mountainous area. It was near Vallon-Pont-d'Arc on the Ardèche River. I looked it up on a map. It was about an hour from the Noel farm.

And as I read more about it, it began to fill me with a longing to see it. I don't know why, but I started to believe that it might, somehow, contain the meaning of life.

Inside the cave, accessed through a tiny hole, were the oldest drawings ever made by human beings. Scientists believed that this cave had been sealed for more than 20,000 years! Their tests showed that some of the art was as old as 32,000 years! It was mind-boggling. On the walls were depictions of animals that had lived there, and among them were lions and rhinoceroses.

Of course, I wanted to go there immediately. But several things held me back. First, stupidly, I was always too busy. Secondly, just as (or perhaps even more) stupidly, I didn't want to return to that area, near the Noels and the one great shame of my life. And most importantly, I couldn't get into the Chauvet even if I went there. The Lascaux Cave had been open to the public for many years, and as a consequence, some of its drawings had been damaged and in some cases destroyed. Over the decades, scientists determined that it was the presence of human beings and specifically their breath that had been the cause. So it was decided that the Chauvet Cave should not be accessible to the general public. Only select scientists and a few academics and historians would ever be allowed into it.

No one, other than that handful of people, has ever seen the drawings inside that marvelous place.

Here, Adam, is your task, the most difficult task of your adventure...an impossible one, I think.

Get into the Chauvet Cave.

See if it contains the meaning of life.

THIRTEEN
CASING THE CHAUVET

"Okay," I said aloud to myself, "how am I going to do this?" I sat there staring at the yellow wall for a moment. Four words kept coming back to me from the letter: *There is danger involved.* What did he mean by that? It almost sounded like he didn't want me to attempt this.

But I had to.

The first thing I needed was more information. Where, exactly, was this place? I got out the map again. I located Arles and looked northward. I couldn't find Vallon-Pont-d'Arc for several minutes, even though I could see that the Ardèche region was just west of the

Rhone Valley. The main highway went up that valley from Arles and Avignon to the city of Lyon. Finally, I found the Ardèche River, and then followed it west from the Rhone and there it was: the village or town of Vallon-Pont-d'Arc. There were no caves marked on the map, but I noticed that on the way to the town there was a large green-colored park with a river running through it, labeled *Réserve Naturelle des Gorges de l'Ardèche.* I could also see from the map's topography that the land was much higher there. All of this looked promising. This was where you would find caves.

I got out my cell and looked up the town, the park, and the Chauvet Cave itself. What was revealed was enticing but not very promising. The town was attractive, a beautiful little place full of old buildings and tourist shops and restaurants. And the park looked spectacular, perfect for canoeing and kayaking, with little beaches here and there. But the cave was something else. It wasn't that it wasn't fascinating. It definitely was. But everything I read about it made my task seem more and more difficult. It didn't look like it would be easy to get to, and just as Grandpa said, there didn't appear to be any public access. I couldn't even find its exact location; it was as if they were hiding it.

It was evening by now, and I had been so intrigued by the letter and my task that I hadn't even taken the time to eat. Feeling depressed about the impossibility of what was before me, I went out to the café I'd been eating at the last few days. I was hoping to see that young waitress again.

I was disappointed at first. She wasn't anywhere in sight, and the woman who came to wait on me was middle-aged and grumpy. She didn't speak a word of English.

"*Américain?*" she barked right away.

"I'll look after him." A much sweeter voice came from inside the restaurant. It was my waitress. She had always seemed shy before and had only spoken short bursts of French, so I was surprised to hear her utter more than a word or two and especially pleased to hear it come out in English.

But I wasn't so pleased with the way she looked. She was obviously finished work for the day, probably on her way home, and though she was nicely dressed in faded cropped jeans that showed off her slim calves, and a bright yellow halter top tied with a ribbon around the neck, her face looked different. I couldn't tell what it was at first. The glow seemed to have left her, or at least the sort of glow that she'd had before. It took me a minute to figure out what it was—she wasn't wearing any makeup. And when she sat down across from me, looking a little pale but smiling, she swept her blond bangs off her forehead and I noticed a little scar on her hairline, almost in the shape of a cross. I have to admit that I had been thinking a lot about her and now, suddenly, she looked awfully ordinary.

"May I sit?"

"Uh, yeah, yeah, sure."

"Shall I order for you again? I do not know your name."

"Uh…" For some reason I was hesitant to give it to her. "Adam," I said finally, "I'm Adam Murphy."

"Well, I am Rose." She turned to the other waitress and ordered something for me. I was sure it would be delicious, like everything else she had ordered for me over the last few days.

"You know," she began, "I have always been wondering, since the time I first see you, who you are."

"Who I am?"

"*Oui.* At first I thought, he is a tourist. But then, where are his parents? Or is he older than his appearance and is vacationing *en Provence* alone?"

"I am seventeen," I lied.

"Really? Maybe." She smiled. "You are *un peu mystérieux*. I like that. Most *Américains*, you know, they are not *mystérieux*, not at all. They are predictable. Very sad. You do wear all those clothes from Aéropostale, so you are a bit, uh, materialistic…buy the things the others buy? Still, you are different too. So I imagined, sometimes, that you were doing something *mystérieux* in Arles, that you were on some sort of *mission dangereuse*." She laughed.

"Well, maybe I am."

She laughed again. "Adam Murphy, I think you are just a nice boy from America and your parents are somewhere nearby, no?"

"Uh…"

"*Mais*, still an *interesting* nice boy." She smiled at me. I was beginning to forget her lack of makeup and that scar. Her personality was awfully attractive, and now that I really checked her out up close, she looked good, makeup or not.

"My parents"—I hated to tell her this—"aren't too far away." Then I added quickly, "But I am really on my own here, no strings attached."

"*Oui?*"

"And I am—kind of—on a dangerous mission. Or, at least, there is something very difficult and unusual that I have to do."

"Tell me!" she exclaimed and patted my hand.

I really didn't want to tell anyone. But for some reason, out it all came, minus the bits about taking the painting, of course. I told her quickly about the first two assignments, just the highlights, then spent lots of time explaining the next task, the one directly in front of me. As I spoke, I realized that I had needed to tell someone what I was doing. I really wasn't sure I could do what my grandfather had asked, and it was kind of freaking me out.

But her face became very serious.

"You cannot do this."

"Pardon me?"

"*La Grotte Chauvet*, it is *un endroit sacré*, a sacred place almost. You cannot just go barging in there. I thought you were not like the other *Américains*?"

"I don't intend to barge in. I won't hurt anybody or anything. I just want to look."

"You just want to accomplish this task! You just want to win. All you want is to be someone important in your grandfather's eyes."

"No."

"*Oui!* And he is dead anyway."

"I-I want to go into the Chauvet Cave because it *is* a sacred place. I want to see those drawings; I want to feel what is special about them. I want to know whatever truth they reveal. I want it to make me a better person."

It was true. And when I said it to her, it kind of shocked me. I wasn't sure I was a very good person, though I had never admitted it out loud to myself before. I knew I was a jerk a lot of the time, but I also knew I was struggling to be the person I should be.

"Really?"

"Really." I swallowed.

The older waitress brought my meal, which was some sort of crepe with cheese and herbs. Rose insisted that I eat and wouldn't have any herself. She watched as I began, knowing I would enjoy what was on my plate. "*Bon appétit!*" she said, her good humor suddenly returning. She sat and watched me for a while. It was a little unnerving. Then she patted my hand again and pushed back her chair. "Well, I must go. If I were you, I would not try to go into La Grotte Chauvet *even* if I was doing it for *la bonne raison.* You should know it is dangerous for you, very dangerous."

"I don't get that. My grandfather said that too."

"But of course it is! The drawings on those walls are the most important art in the world. They are easily destroyed. The presence of too many person damages them. They are well protected. The authorities will do *anything* to protect them. Getting in is impossible! And if you are found in there, I don't know what they would do to you. You would need a good—how do you call it?—lawyer?"

"Lawyer?" I gulped.

"*Mais oui. En France*, we take art seriously. Despite your age, you might not get back to America for a very, very long time."

I stopped eating.

"Besides," she added, getting up and smiling at me, "the meaning of life, Adam, it is not in that cave. It is somewhere else."

She was gone before I could ask her what she meant by that. She vanished down the street like a ghost. I finished my meal, paid and returned to my room. I wanted to be in bed early tonight. I wanted to get up first thing tomorrow morning and make my way to Vallon-Pont-d'Arc. I was going to need all my wits about me when I got there. I felt like a thief readying himself to check out the lay of the land before the big job.

Though Grandpa had said that the cave was in the Ardèche region, about an hour away, that was only true if you were leaving from the Noels' home and moving across country as the crow flies. It took me closer to two hours to get there. I had to take a cab up the highway past the city of Avignon and then farther north on the big road toward Lyon. About halfway up, we turned west and soon reached the *Réserve Naturelle* that I'd seen on the map. The Ardèche River flowed through it like a blue snake, and the road wound along above it at the top of a massive gorge. I was surprised at the heavy traffic. This was obviously a popular tourist area. It wasn't hard to see why. Everything was just *so* stunningly beautiful and the views were incredible. I thought of how this was so unlike back home, and for some reason that made me think of Leon and how much he would love to have the chance to see this. I stared down into the gorge at the dots of canoes and kayaks and the little beaches, beige and gray, sandy and rocky. Just after we'd passed through the park, the Pont d'Arc itself came into view: a famous tourist spot on the river that I'd seen on the reserve's website. It was about a million years old, a rock formation that actually formed a huge bridge! There were even trees growing on it. It rose about thirty yards above the river, like some sort of prehistoric animal stretching itself over the water. I gazed down onto the sheer limestone cliffs below, green about two thirds of the way up with lush trees and plants, but light brown, almost yellow, near their tops. Was the great cave out there somewhere, in one of these mountains? That snapped me out of my tourist dream. *Danger.* That's what Grandpa had said. And when Rose explained why, it made a lot of sense. The other tasks were difficult—but this one could get me into very deep trouble. I was nearing the beginning of my most daunting mission. My stomach started to churn.

We got closer to the river as we approached Vallon-Pont-d'Arc and soon were traveling through some dark little tunnels cut right into the gorge. It barely seemed like there was enough room for two cars to pass.

I had asked the driver to leave me in the village. That seemed like the best place to start. I had to find out exactly where the cave was, ask discreetly, and never give away what I really wanted.

The town was a little smaller than I imagined, but it was gorgeous. It was ancient, of course, with narrow streets and low stone walls and many stone buildings. Quite a few of the buildings had half-pipe shingles on their roofs and the little shops had colorful awnings. There were lots of flowers and trees, some of them kind of like the palm trees we have in Florida. The whole place was so tightly packed that it was almost claustrophobic. But it was awfully impressive too, like being on the set of a historical film, a romantic one, I guess, maybe a chick flick. Something I could take Vanessa to, or maybe Shirley. That would probably be better. The little sidewalks were filled with people and the cutesy stores were jammed with tourists. Unfortunately, I could often tell which ones were American. They were talking to the French the way I had at first—loudly and slowly.

I figured that a place like this would have a tourist kiosk, and I asked to be dropped off there. Sure enough, it was in an old stone building in a sort of courtyard in the center of the town. A big wooden door that looked like it had been made for a castle was wide open, and people were pouring in and out of the building, women's heels clicking on the heavily polished wood floor. I had to wait in line for a while. The woman who finally spoke to me from behind the counter was probably in her thirties, slim, with dark hair cut in a fashionable short style. She was wearing subtle makeup and smelled awfully good.

"*Américain?*" she asked. That was the first of several depressing things she said. I had thought I was at least a bit different from the other Americans.

"I am looking for some information about the Chauvet Cave."

"You cannot go there," she said very quickly and firmly. Then she smiled. "May I help you with anything else?"

"I-I don't want to go there, of course. I know it isn't open to the public—"

"That is correct."

"But—"

"Anything else, sir?"

"Can you just tell me where it is?"

"Why would you want to know that?"

"Just so I can see it from a distance."

"But there is nothing to see from a distance." She flashed her wonderful smile again. "There is much to do in Vallon-Pont-d'Arc itself and, of course, even more in the surrounding area. This region of l'Ardèche is one of the most beautiful natural places on the earth. You can hike, canoe or kayak, or simply—"

"I am not a hiker or a kayaker. But thank you."

I thought she gave me a bit of a suspicious look as I stepped away from the counter. I noticed that a few of the other employees had glanced my way when I persisted with my questions. It was obvious that the official line in the area was to not encourage average people or tourists to be curious about the cave. But I wasn't an average person or a tourist, not now.

I *had* to get close to the cave. In fact, *all* I had to do for now was to get close, just see it, do that thief-checking-out-the-lay-of-the-land thing. I had to figure out how in the world I might get in there.

The instant I was back on the street, it occurred to me that perhaps the regular citizens of Vallon-Pont-d'Arc wouldn't have the same reluctance about revealing the cave's location. So I plucked up my courage and entered the nearest patisserie. There were quite a few of them in the little town, despite its size. The French certainly liked their baking and their pastries. I figured the owners of these businesses were constantly dealing with American tourists, so they might be able to understand me.

It smelled like heaven inside—fresh-baked bread and sugar and chocolate and cinnamon and all sorts of good things. It was a quaint place, of course, with lots of wood and stone, as rustic and old as they could make it. The man behind the cash register looked as though he'd been eating quite a few of his own wares. He wore a chef's hat, likely for the tourists.

"*Excusez moi, monsieur,*" I began. "*S'il vous plait, où est la grotte du Chauvet?*"

The fat man looked at me for a long while, as if he were trying to figure out which kind of *pain aux chocolate* I wanted.

"*Pardon?*" he finally said. I guess my accent wasn't that good.

"The Chauvet Cave?"

"Ah!" he exclaimed with a smile. "La Grotte Chauvet! Go to le Pont d'Arc, maybe two mile from the town, yes? It is on the road *à la direction de la Réserve Naturelle.* Then, go up."

"Up?"

"Up to the cliffs. *Comprenez-vous?*"

"*Oui. Merci beaucoup, monsieur.*"

That was all I got. But it was enough.

Thinking it unwise to ask anyone to take me there, I walked. Or at least I thought I would walk. Before I was too far out of town, already into the countryside (which appeared almost immediately), a little car pulled over. It roared like a chainsaw... a small one. There was a kayak about twice the length of the vehicle strapped to the roof.

"*Américain?*" the driver asked. He was a young guy, maybe a year or two older than me, wearing peach-colored shorts, a beaded turquoise necklace, sandals and no shirt. The Black Keys were playing on his iPod; I could hear the bass line pulsing right through his earbuds.

"*Oui.*"

"*Parlez-vous français?*"

"*Un peu.*" It sounded to me like I'd said "a poo."

"Where are you going?"

"Can you take me to le Pont d'Arc?"

"*Mais oui, monsieur! Bien sur!*"

I got in, and he didn't say another word for the next two or three minutes as we careened at top speed along the little, curving road, past beautiful country houses, vineyards and fields, small tourist businesses, through those cool tunnels along the river, then to a large parking lot, dressed up with all sorts of trees and flowers to not look like a parking lot.

"*Voilà!*" said my new friend and immediately leaped from his little sardine can and began taking his kayak down. He acted as though we'd known each other for a while and he had simply given me a lift and then gone about his business. I considered asking him about the Chauvet Cave but decided against it. The parking lot was filled with people, many unloading canoes or kayaks or returning with them from the river. I had a hundred other candidates to choose from. I could pick the perfect one.

A gravel walkway led down from the parking lot to the Pont d'Arc. I could see it from where I stood. Though I wanted to get on with my quest, the sight of it stopped me in my tracks. I had rarely seen anything as beautiful. I'm not a big believer in God, or at least I don't think I am—haven't figured that out yet—but if God didn't make that giant bridge, then I don't know who or what did. The water was like glass and as blue as the sky. Kayaks and canoes glided on it as paddlers stared up at this magnificent creation.

I shook myself away from it and turned back to the lot. Mostly, I heard French voices, though there were a few other languages I wasn't sure about, and here and there, shouts in English, both British and American. Then I heard something that really caught my attention.

"Hey, man, let's get moving, eh!"

The guy was wearing a Toronto Maple Leafs T-shirt and khaki shorts, and his skin was tanned like leather. The dude he was yelling at was similarly bronzed, sporting a Molson Canadian beer shirt, kind of dragging himself behind, looking like he'd had too many glasses of his favorite brew during the lunch hour. They were heading down the gravel path to the water, where they had probably docked their boat. *Canadians.* It looked like they had been in the Ardèche for a while, taking in the sun. They were probably in their early twenties.

I would never admit this to anyone else, but I knew from experience that Canadians were a lot more international in their outlook than Americans. It always shocked me when I heard my cousins really get rolling in a conversation, not only about things that were happening in their own country, but also in America (though they always called it "the United States") as well as in Europe and South America and even Africa, for God's sake. My buddies and I back home had enough trouble keeping informed about local politics! They didn't know *anything* about the Great White North, even though Canuck-land was just a few miles away over the border. I remember correcting them when they referred to Canada's president, instead of prime minister.

So, I figured these two guys at Pont d'Arc might have actually found out something about the Ardèche region before they came here. Americans, of course, rarely did that before they traveled. We just showed up. Canadians were usually pretty friendly too. I stepped toward them.

"Hey, guys!" I shouted.

The first one, the guy in the Leafs shirt, was looking back toward his friend. But he turned around, saw me and answered right away.

"Hey, man. American, right?"

God, even the Canucks can pick us out over here.

"Yeah, from Buffalo."

"Oh…man, I'm sorry to hear that," he said straight-faced. Then he smiled. "Just kidding!" He slapped me on the shoulder.

"You guys been here for a while?"

"Good guess, Sherlock," said the Molson dude, coming up from behind.

"You ever heard of the Chauvet Cave?"

"Sure," said Maple Leaf, "it's right up there." He pointed slightly to the northeast and up the cliffs. "Checked it out before we came over, found the exact location on a satellite map, pretty interesting."

Bingo.

"But you can't go there," Maple Leaf said.

"I know."

"We're here for the kayaking, man, and the babes."

"And the wine," said Molson.

"What if I wanted to go up there? How would I do it? I just want to see it from a distance." Every Canadian I ever met pretty much minded his own business. It was a national characteristic. These guys would never ask me exactly why I was interested in the Chauvet Cave.

"There's a path that leads right from the lot here," Maple Leaf offered right away. "It isn't marked. It's all very secret, you know, *une place sacrée*." He laughed.

"But if you walk over there"—he pointed at a spot at the far end of the lot—"and look into the shrubs, you'll see it. It's the only path at that end of the lot. It'll take you up to a place where the scientists work. They get there by a little road that goes off the main one a little ways back. We had a brewski in town with one of the tall foreheads working there. He wouldn't say much about it, but he told us about another path that leads from their buildings up to the cliffs. It takes you to the cave. He made a point of telling us that it was sealed off and under surveillance."

"But we aren't interested anyway," said Molson. "Too many girls and too much boating going on. I mean"—he looked up at the blue, sunny sky— "check out the rays, man. And besides, I hear they're pretty strict about protecting that cave. We'd rather spend our time out here"—he motioned at the gorgeous Pont d'Arc and the river—"in the company of *les femmes*, than in some French jail."

"Adiós, Americano!" said Maple Leaf, and off they went.

I watched them walk away, wondering if it was advisable to even look for the trail without learning more about what exactly was up ahead. But I wasn't about to turn back now. At least, I reasoned, I can check out the buildings. I'll make a decision about what to do when I get there.

I was surprised at how quickly the buildings came into view. I must have walked uphill for about three or four minutes, tops, and there they were, in an opening off a small road, with a compact parking lot. The buildings weren't fancy; they looked like housing for the military, a group of concrete structures with barely a sign. I guess that made sense. It wasn't as if they appeared to be trying to hide anything— they just weren't looking to attract attention. There were about a dozen cars in the little lot. As I stood there, a good hundred feet away, a car pulled up and a man got out, wearing glasses and sporting a frizzy hairstyle that could be best described as neglected. He was dressed in brown shoes, beige pants and a short-sleeved, green-and-white-checked shirt, an awfully boring look for a Frenchman. He was carrying a big briefcase and didn't even notice me as he slammed his door, locked it and marched off across the lot toward the front entrance to the biggest building, his head down, muttering to himself. At the door, he was greeted by a man in a uniform.

After they'd smiled at one another and exchanged a little conversation, the unfashionable guy headed off into the building and the other man, the one in the uniform, turned and looked right at me. I expected it to be just a glance, but he seemed to notice that I was looking his way and stepped out from the doorway and stared at me. I moved back down the trail I'd come up.

But I didn't go very far. Once I was almost out of sight, I squatted down and peered through the under-brush at the man. After a few seconds, he re-entered the building.

The Canadians had said that the path that led up to the cave was on the other side of these structures. As I got up from my crouch, I could actually see what I thought was the path in the distance, or at least its outline through the underbrush on the far side of one of the buildings, winding its way up the cliffs, then disappearing where it met a field of fruit trees. There were woods beyond that and the sheer limestone cliffs in the distance. Could that really be the path? Vanishing into a field and then into the woods?

I decided that if I left the lower path I was on and plunged into the trees, I would come out on the little road that led to the parking lot, far out of sight of the guard or whatever he was. I really didn't think he would be able to see me. Then I could crouch down and move through more trees until I was at the far side of the buildings, and pick up the path to the cave on the other side.

I felt a little ridiculous, given that I was sure there was no law against being near the scientists' buildings—you just couldn't go in without an invitation. People must have meandered by here from time to time. They probably even got much closer to the cave than this. And I doubted the guard would do anything other than watch me if I reappeared in the parking lot. But I didn't *want* him watching me, not given what I intended to do in the very near future. There was no way I could take the chance of him recognizing me. That might make things very difficult at a delicate moment.

So I sneaked through the trees, up the little road, around the buildings and, sure enough, found a path. I made certain I was out of sight of the buildings before I left the trees and got onto the trail. It was relatively flat here. There was the field up ahead, revealed now as a vineyard. It was curious to think that someone owned this l

part of it this close to the legendar

The path didn't stop at the vir

wound around it and then headed

entered the woods. I tramped through

to every little sound, wondering at times if the bird

calls were signals from security people who were

watching me and about to swoop down and arrest me.

But that seemed ridiculous.

The path was narrow and certainly not well marked, but that made sense. I'd worn my hiking boots and could hear the twigs and pebbles crunching under my feet. It was a warm day and I was starting to sweat. Soon I came to a place where I could rest— a rocky ledge that stuck out from the cliffs. It was amazing. You could look down over the gorge from here. I saw the scientists' buildings, their little parking lot, the bigger parking lot, the river and the Pont d'Arc far below. But I didn't want to pause for long. The steep path led onward and upward, through underbrush and into the cliffs.

Off I went. But after ten or fifteen minutes of walking, much of it still steeply upward, I was ready to stop. I was beginning to doubt that this was the way.

all, I had no proof, just the words of a couple of Canadians who had a drink with a scientist. Perhaps he had purposely given them the wrong information.

But then I heard something. In fact, I heard *someone.* He was whistling.

I was exhausted and had been walking with my head down, not looking more than a few yards in front of me. I didn't bother to raise my head now. I quickly left the trail, almost jumping into the underbrush, and scurried a good ten feet away. I crouched down. Only then did I slowly turn and raise my gaze up the cliff in the direction I had been heading. Almost directly above me and no more than half a dozen car lengths away, I saw a man dressed in what looked like gray-blue coveralls, wearing a white hard hat with a light attached to it, sitting on a large plastic container in a tiny open cave. He appeared to be waiting for someone. I looked away from him and my gaze followed the path past him. It narrowed and became a wooden walkway. And then I saw it.

Thirty feet or so farther along, the walkway ended in four smooth, expertly-surfaced stone steps. The steps led into the cliff. Right into it! I took a chance and moved forward a little so I could see better.

I could now make out that the steps led up to an opening, and in that opening was a huge steel door, built right into the cliff! It was like a portal to a magical world.

Then I heard voices. I dropped to the ground. Several people were coming up the path behind me toward the man in the little open cave! There were about five or six of them, all dressed in those gray-blue coveralls, all with helmets and lamps. As they neared, they came within a few feet of me. I held my breath. They were chatting happily, a sense of excitement in their conversation. Mostly it was in French, but it was interspersed with bits and pieces of English. It was obvious to me that they were talking about the cave, mostly because they were using all sorts of big, scientific words. I noticed that the guard from the buildings was with them. He was now dressed in those coveralls too and was leading the way, not saying anything. They must be about to enter the cave!

As I looked up, one of the men caught my eye. He was the most animated of the group and used the least scientific vocabulary. He was making fun of some of the things the other men were saying and offering comments about the weather, the beautiful day, the smells and sounds. Their conversation was sprinkled with enough English for me to understand. He was much taller than the rest and his curly blond hair cascaded down his shoulders. A goatee grew wildly from his chin, extending almost halfway down his chest. He wore a pair of circular sunglasses, the frames a startling yellow-and-purple pattern, and I noticed a bright red shirt under his coveralls. He was teasing the only female, a young woman wearing black, horn-rimmed glasses and a short haircut. I could see that she was nervously fiddling with her hair, as if to make it presentable under her helmet. Some of the man's comments made her blush and look down at the ground. It was obvious that the blond man was a very different sort from the others. At one point, he pretended to run toward the cave, as if he were making a break for it and attempting to get in without clearance. Though some of the others laughed, the guard didn't.

They approached the man sitting on the container just inside the little cave to the side of the walkway and spent a few moments talking with him. Soon he unlocked the big container, drew out strange-looking shoes and foot-wide square lights attached to battery packs on belts, handed them out and then let the whole party by. When they had gone, he trudged down the path, right by me, obviously on his way back to the buildings. Luckily, he didn't spot me.

The group grew silent as they neared the main cave at the end of the wooden walkway. Even the blond man didn't say anything. I edged out to the path, peered up through the underbrush and watched them. Now I could see that there was a key pad on the wall next to that magical steel door and above it was a surveillance camera! My heart sank.

The guard punched in a complicated code— about twenty numbers that he touched with lightning speed. It was apparent that only he knew that code. Then he opened the door. I leaned forward, my face completely exposed, and as I did, the man with the colorful glasses turned around. I pulled my head back. I didn't think he saw me. But he looked my way for a moment, shook his head and then turned back toward the cave door. From where I was, I couldn't see much inside the door, just a dark opening as each and every member of the group entered it with a sort of quiet reverence. As they stepped through the opening, they all put on the special shoes the man had handed out. When they went into the cave, it seemed as though they walked downward. Then the door closed and they were gone. It was as if they had disappeared into another dimension.

I crouched there for a long time, listening to the near-silence: just the wind, the songs of a few birds, and the sound of moving water barely audible far below. Then I got to my feet and walked up past the little cave where the man had sat on the container, along the narrow wooden walkway, and toward the door. It was indeed steel, not much taller than me and not particularly wide. Well aware of the surveillance camera, I didn't come close. I imagined what the scientists were seeing in there.

How in the world was I going to get in?

FOURTEEN
THE KEY TO THE CHAUVET

As I rode back through the beautiful Ardèche in a cab I had hailed in Vallon, I thought about my situation. At first, it seemed impossible. But then I started to think, really think. Grandpa often said there was always a way to do something, no matter how difficult it was to accomplish. All you had to do was work at it and use your imagination. Perhaps that was what he was trying to teach me right now.

It took me almost all the way to Arles, but eventually it came to me.

The cave was heavily fortified and protected. But there were people who did get into it. The scientists or the other experts, the men and women who worked in those buildings lower down in the gorge. *They* went in and out every day.

There was only one way to enter the Chauvet. I had to go in *with* them.

When I got back to my hotel I started to consider how I could possibly do that. Then I remembered the blond guy, the one who seemed so different from the others, so unconcerned about the rules.

By the time I went to bed that night I had a plan. I'd bought a few postcards in Vallon, so I wrote one to Vanessa. I'd do the one for Shirley later, and the one for Leon. I needed my sleep. I set my cell-phone alarm to wake me very early the next morning and slipped under the covers.

✿

Despite the early hour, my waitress was at the café when I arrived. She was wearing nothing but a very long white T-shirt with some kind of a design on the front, a skinny belt and tennis shoes and just a dash of makeup to make her look fabulous. As she approached, the drawing on her shirt became clear— *The Little Prince.* She had worn it for me.

She smiled at me and said, "You are still alive and not in jail, so you must not have tried to enter la Grotte Chauvet?"

"No. I'll do that today."

She looked concerned. "Remember, you do not have to do it."

"Yes, I do." I tried to say it with conviction, but it didn't come out that way.

She leaned down and squeezed my hand. "No, you do not."

I wanted to kiss her. Not on the mouth, not like she was my girlfriend or anything, but like she was a friend. Despite my relationship with Shirley and my interest in Vanessa, I wanted to kiss this French girl in Arles. It was kind of confusing.

❉

I was in the cab on the highway up to the Ardèche before eight o'clock, so nervous that I couldn't keep my legs from shaking. This time, I had the cabdriver drop me at the Pont d'Arc parking lot. As I had suspected, there weren't many people there yet. Tourists aren't exactly early risers. So I sat down and waited. The people I wanted to see arrived about an hour later.

"Hey!" I called out to the two Canadians, who seemed to be wearing the same shirts they had on yesterday.

I cut to the chase. Last night, when I was going over the events of the day trying to figure out how the heck I might get into the cave, I had thought about these guys and the fact that the scientist they had been drinking with had told them stuff no one else would talk about. I believed that they'd been speaking to the guy with the long blond hair, and that he was perfect for me and my mission.

When I described him, they agreed that it was the same guy and told me where they had met him.

I walked to Vallon and found the café. By the time I got there, it was past prime breakfast hour, but not so late that my target wouldn't be there. I guessed— correctly—that he liked to take his time in the mornings. Sure enough, there he was: long blond hair falling toward the table, yellow-and-purple-rimmed sunglasses on, lenses black as night, low on his nose.

A thick, well-thumbed paperback sat on his little table in front of his drink, and he had his head down, writing in a lined notebook. His long goatee actually touched the pad as he wrote.

I noticed that almost everyone in the half-full café kept stealing glances at him. The waitresses paid him particular attention.

I wasn't surprised to find out that he was friendly. When I came up to introduce myself, he whipped off his glasses, looked up and instantly asked me to join him. (I didn't give him my real name, just to be on the safe side. I called myself Bernard McLean.) He was younger than I expected, but the most notable thing about him up close was his eyes. They blazed at me, even though I had said nothing remarkable to him, nor was I—obviously—remarkable myself. It was as if his eyes were always lit up like that. An extraordinary energy came from him, an undeniable charisma.

I also wasn't surprised that he spoke English. His cool French accent didn't make his conversation difficult to follow: he had a way of almost caressing words. I imagined he could make them sound interesting in any language. He was a man of quick movements and thoughts. He examined me closely, as if learning every inch of my face, penetrating it and getting into my brain.

"So you are doing some work up at the Chauvet Cave?" I asked.

Those eyes twinkled. "How do you know that, American?"

"I saw you."

"Yes, you were hiding in the bushes, watching."

He *had* seen me.

"I have something I need to do there."

"Need to, eh? Sounds like a mission." He grinned. "*Une mission dangereuse?*"

"Yes, in fact."

"Tell me."

As I've mentioned, I'm a pretty good storyteller, just like Grandpa. And I really gave this tale all that I had. The heartbreaking story of a grandfather who desperately wants his dying wish fulfilled, for all the right reasons. What was interesting about this guy's reaction was how intrigued he seemed to be, and not just by the story, but by how I told it. He looked not only fascinated but genuinely amused. Those eyes sparkled and his eyebrows seemed to go up and down with the rhythms of my story. He looked like he knew when the climax was coming and anticipated it with great excitement.

"*Merveilleux!*" he exclaimed when I was done, so loudly that the whole café turned to him. I gave him a look that indicated I wanted us to be quieter.

"*Oui*," he whispered, "*une mission très dangereuse.*" He winked at me.

"Can you help me?"

"Help you get into la Grotte Chauvet? That is impossible—"

"But I—"

He leaned forward and spoke so quietly that I could barely hear him. "Which is exactly why I think we should try!"

I could barely believe what he had said.

"Really?"

"Really. You are now in the hands of Mermoz!"

The name was obviously supposed to mean something to me. He said it almost like a kid might, if he were telling you that he was the best player on his football team. I glanced around the café again. Every patron in the restaurant, and the owner and waitresses too, were sneaking peeks our way. The women seemed especially interested. It was beginning to dawn on me that I was sitting with an important man, but an awfully strange one.

"What—what do you do, sir, for a living?" I asked.

"Anarchist!" he shouted. There were a few giggles around us.

"Anarchist?"

"Communist!"

"Communist?"

"Rebel extraordinaire. And I write books." He smiled. Now a few people nearby laughed out loud.

"You are an author?"

"I prefer artist or storyteller."

"Like Antoine de Saint-Exupéry?"

I thought his face was going to split with happiness. "*Oui! Oui!* Like *le géant de la France*! I am Mermoz! And you and I"—he lowered his voice again—"we have a wonderful story to create now. We are going to invent the story of the only boy to ever enter la Grotte Chauvet! But there is danger!"

"So I have heard."

"And romance!"

"Romance?"

"Well, of a sort. This whole notion is romantic and thrilling and dramatic! Add to all of this the fact that, by good fortune, we have an added element that creates a good deal of tension."

"Added element?"

"Time!"

"Time?"

"Tomorrow is the last day of a fifteen-day period when the scientists and special invitees are allowed into the cave. Human beings cannot be in there any longer than that or our presence, our very breath, might do damage to the cave drawings, you know. There will not be another such period for many months. And I, Mermoz, storyteller and documenter in literary arts, am one of those, invited by the president himself to tell the story of the inside of la Grotte Chauvet. Don't you see? We, therefore, have a clock on our story, sir. Oh, that is always a delicious thing! We must get you in and out of the cave by tomorrow. We have but twenty-four hours! That is a fabulous ingredient in our tale! It creates tension, my young American friend!"

He said the last sentence with a loud flourish and then looked sheepish. "I am getting too excited," he said quietly. "Now, this is how I envision this story, this tale of the American boy entering la Grotte Chauvet against all odds." He paused for a second.

"I must tell you, however, if this does not work out as we plan, if you are found out while on the way to the cave or inside it, you must promise me here and now—on the watery grave of St. Ex—that you will swear that you have never met me, that I in no way helped you and that you will take your punishment, whatever it is, like a man, and suffer whatever the French authorities decide to do with you, without accusing me…Mermoz!"

"I-I suppose so."

"You suppose?"

"I-I promise." I didn't have any choice.

"I am the good guy in the story…but I can be the villain too."

"Yes," I said, though I didn't like the sound of that.

"If you are caught, I shall disavow all knowledge of you. In fact, I will pursue you along with the authorities and recommend your arrest."

"Really?"

"But I must! Don't you see it? Ah, it would be a marvelous twist to the end of our tale! Very European!" His face grew serious. "But we shall not wish for that as our denouement. We shall do all we can to make this a happy tale, an American drama full of spills and chills with an American ending—which means a dull ending, but nevertheless, it must be done."

"I hope so."

"This, Monsieur McLean, is what we shall do!"

Though I was entering into this bargain with some concern, I was awfully pleased too. I had calculated correctly. I had stumbled upon possibly the only man who had ever been inside the Chauvet Cave who would find it exciting to break the rules and help someone else sneak in or, in this case, actually participate in such a crime.

"But," he said, "before I begin, stand up please."

It wasn't what I wanted to hear at that moment. I was anxious to hear him tell our story—the spine-tingling tale of how he was going to get me into the forbidden cave. I wanted the details and I wanted them now.

But he insisted. He smiled and motioned for me to get to my feet. I stood up. First, he looked down at my shoes and put one of his beside one of mine, as if comparing. Then he leaned forward, his face coming within inches of mine. He had done almost the same thing while we were sitting. He was one of those people who like to get inside your personal space. It was a bit unnerving.

But this time, he didn't say anything. In fact, after he examined me for a while, our eyes at exactly the same height, he nodded his head as if confirming something, slapped his spectacular glasses back onto his face, turned abruptly and walked away.

"Meet me first thing tomorrow morning, about eight o'clock, in the parking lot of the scientists' buildings," he barked over his shoulder. In seconds he was at the door. He opened it with a shove and exited. It sprang back and slammed. Many of the café patrons were staring at him as he left. I was suddenly alone at his table, left to pay his bill, suspended in that frustrating and yet fascinating moment, sort of like at the end of a chapter in a novel when the author has primed his readers into a state of excitement but then pauses before he reveals what happens next.

FIFTEEN
INTO THE GREAT CAVE

I was there exactly on time. And so was Mermoz. In fact, he was sitting in his car—another battered old Citroën—completely naked. Or at least, he appeared to be. He was looking around to make sure no one was watching, and his hand was covering his face as he motioned to me with just a slight movement of his head. I reluctantly opened the door and got in. I say "reluctantly" for obvious reasons. I was wondering if he was some kind of a pervert. But I was big and strong and confident in my ability to protect myself and, more importantly, at this moment he was the only way I could get into the Chauvet Cave. The *only* way.

And besides, he was a famous writer. How weird could he be? That seemed like a stupid question almost the moment I thought it.

It turned out that he wasn't naked. He was wearing a small hat…and a pair of boxer shorts.

He was also completely bald. And I mean completely. He hadn't one strand of hair left on his head, or on his chin, for that matter. Because his hand had been over his face, I hadn't noticed his brand-new cue-ball look when I first saw him through the car door. I had also been mesmerized, once again, by his eyes. He wasn't wearing his spectacular sunglasses. Those brilliant blue peepers had locked on me the instant they saw me and that was really all I had looked at.

"But you're—" I said.

He held up his hand to silence me. "This," he said, "is our plan, our—shall we say—story." He inhaled deeply, exhaled and then paused. "I noticed yesterday, that you, my extraordinarily tall young American friend, are exactly the same height as Mermoz."

That was what the eyeball-to-eyeball stare had been all about.

"Mermoz is also a remarkably attractive and young-looking man, just like yourself."

Okay, that was weird. I wanted to disagree, but he was kind of right.

"Our story begins with those facts as its launching mechanism."

Then he told me his idea, our plan. It seemed fraught with problems and yet the more I thought about it, the more it appealed to me. It was imaginative, to say the least, as unbelievable as a work of fiction in some places, and very dangerous in others (which certainly gave me pause). But wild as it was, it just might work. That was all that mattered at that moment. So I agreed to do it.

He reached down below the seat and brought up a plastic bag, which contained a blond goatee, unmistakably the beard of the great Mermoz, and many curly blond locks of long hair, unmistakably the former property of his head. I had thought that he had shaved himself bald. But the great Mermoz really *was* bald! He handed me the bag. "Do not tell anyone!" he muttered. Then he reached into the backseat to retrieve a pile of clothing. His unique sunglasses sat on top. "I have more than one pair," he said with a smile.

Half an hour later, I was walking up the trail toward the cave with the other scientists, wearing the blue-gray coveralls issued only to those few fortunate individuals allowed into the sacred Chauvet space. On my head was a white helmet, complete with a light. The whole thing was strapped tightly around my chin. Mermoz's long blond wig was pushed down over my own hair, his goatee stuck to my chin, and his dark glasses were on my face, adjusted tightly to stay put. As instructed, I had my head down and was saying absolutely nothing, even when others addressed me.

"Another one of those days for the great Mermoz?" asked one of the scientists.

"He's a weird one," whispered another.

As Mermoz had helped me get into disguise in his little car—a not inconsiderable feat—he had coached me.

"I am known as a moody sort, my young American friend, some say a manic depressive, but I say not! Mermoz is merely an artist! Some days I am the life of the party, while other times I do not speak, at all, to anyone. Some days I keep my head down and my thoughts to myself. They have seen me like that once or twice already this season." He brought his fingers to his lips and kissed them. "It is perfect! You are my size, disguised as me with my hair and beard, my spectacles, my special-issue coveralls and hat, and you are young and beautiful like me…and you can remain silent!"

He had taught me to say just one phrase, and to say it exactly as he did: "*Je ne parle pas aujourd'hui.*" I am not talking today.

But that was just part of his plan. The rest of it really worried me. I was turning it over in my mind as I walked up the hill, my heart pounding. In fact, my anxiety was almost overshadowing the fact that I was about to enter the legendary Chauvet Cave, about to see if it contained the meaning of life, about to fulfill the most difficult assignment my grandfather could give me. Finally I would live up to his expectations. If I did this—and it grew nearer with every step—I would certainly no longer be just "okay." I would be a worthy McLean.

But could I actually pull this off? Would the secu-rity guy (who was walking farther back in the group) figure it out? Was I insane to go along with Mermoz's bizarre plan, something right out of a novel? It was only going to get tougher from here.

The rest of his plan, the last part, kept bothering me.

"Should you be successful," Mermoz had said in the car, "I shall drive the getaway car!" His face lit up with excitement. "I will meet you in the parking lot afterward and take you, at high speed, back down the mountain and to your lodgings! Where, by the way, are you staying?"

I hesitated. "I…I won't need you to take me all the way. Just drive me to Vallon and I will get home by myself."

Mermoz nodded with a twinkle in his eye. "You are a smart boy. Keep such information close to your chest!"

"And what if I'm not successful?"

A dark cloud came over the famous author's face. "There will be shouting and a pursuit! I will hear it and race up the trail and help the authorities capture you! You will find Mermoz like a lion to deal with in this situation."

I believed him.

"Once we have you in custody, I shall explain that you sneaked into my room while I was asleep, tied me down, drugged me and stole my precious Chauvet clothing. You chose to disguise yourself as the Great Mermoz!"

"Will they believe that?"

"When I tell it, they shall! And you, sir, are a maniac! That is the role you will be cast into if they catch you. A crazy American intent upon getting into the sacred French cave! Just as others have tried to damage our *Mona Lisa* in the Louvre! And, believe me, I will leave clear evidence of what you have done."

"But why would you do that? You would betray me?"

"Because that is the European ending to the story, as I told you. The tragedy of you." Then his face became serious. "But also because if it were known that I helped you get into la Grotte Chauvet, my reputation would be in tatters. I cannot have that."

"Then why are you doing this? Why take this risk?"

"Ah, that is exactly why. The risk! The excitement! The story! One must have adventure in every aspect, every moment, of life. If you can accomplish this, I will live the rest of my life knowing that I put *you* into the sacred cave! It will be our delicious secret. Ah! *C'est formidable*! If you are not successful, it will all be extremely exciting too. I cannot lose!"

But *I* could.

❖

Up we continued toward the cave. Had I made a deal with the devil? Mermoz might be a genius, but he was a nutbar too.

We stopped briefly to see the man sitting in the small open cave, with the equipment for the scientists. He gave us all antiseptic cave shoes, panel lights and battery belts. I remembered Mermoz looking down at my feet in the café yesterday, placing one of his beside mine and seeing that they were exactly the same size. He had thought of everything.

We moved out. As we neared the Chauvet Cave, my heart raced. Soon the steel door came into view. It seemed even more like a portal to a great imaginary world now. Once the scientists in front of me were within a few steps of it, they stopped. The security guy made his way past all of us. When he slipped by me, he glanced at my face. It seemed to me that he did a slight double take. But he walked on. He punched the numbers into the keypad at lightning speed again and then moved to the door. I tried not to look up at the surveillance camera. He turned the lock and pushed the entrance open. Imagine, I thought, if I can do this, get in and out without anyone knowing! I was fourth in the line and couldn't see clearly past the others. All I could make out inside was absolute darkness. The first scientist entered, sat down and put on his clean shoes and then appeared to immediately descend.

I could hear his boots banging on what sounded like a metal staircase. Then the second scientist made his way in and then the third.

Then it was my turn.

I took a deep breath.

I approached the opening. I couldn't see much even here, just the flashing helmet lights of the other scientists in the darkness in front of me. I sat down and put on my cave shoes. I'd worn my runners today, just in case I might have to move at top speed at some point. I threw them behind me on the path. Then I pushed myself up, felt my feet touch a metal step and lowered my head so my light illuminated my way in the darkness. I descended four or five steps, reached a short flat stretch, then turned and descended more stairs before the path flattened out again. I was on the metal walkway inside the Chauvet Cave, advancing into it! I couldn't believe it. I began to sweat as adrenaline surged through me.

The cavern was huge, its ceiling high above my head. I had a sense of being in another time and space, another world. The metal walkway, which had rails designed to keep even these renowned scientists away from the floor and the walls and whatever was on them, wound around in front of me, leading deeper into the cave. It was beyond eerie. The blackness was only illuminated in the circles of light made by our head-lamps and the squares thrown by the panel lights we carried, showing amazing rock formations on the cave's walls, stalagmites sticking up from the floor and stalactites looking like the big icicles that appear in Buffalo in the winter. But these strange shapes were made by the centuries-old drippings of mineral solutions instead of ice.

There was little sound in the cavity, just the clang of our shoes on the metal walkway. The scientists, many of whom had been in here before, still seemed awed by their surroundings. No one said a word. It was like being in a church, the greatest, spookiest cathedral in the world.

The whole thing was almost too much for me. I was inside a dream. Everything was brown and white and gray, and looked like nothing I had ever seen or even imagined. I doubted that the surface of Mars could be more exotic. My heart kept pumping hard. I had a weird thought: if I could bring Leon here someday, would it cure him?

This cave had been sealed for over 20,000 years and some of the drawings were more than 100 centuries older than that! That meant they existed in the days of Neanderthals, days when (as this cave proved) rhinoceroses, wild horses and lions roamed in southern France. I was back in history and yet in no age at all, suspended in time. I could hardly wait to see the drawings, to feast my eyes (as *no* kid had in 32,000 years!) on the first known art made by human beings. I was ready to discover the meaning of life. It really felt like that was about to happen.

I knew we would see some cave art soon, and that wasn't just a sixth sense. I had studied the Chauvet on the French Ministry of Culture's website on my cell back at the hotel. They'd posted an interior map. I was certain we were just steps away from entering the part of the cavity called the Brunel Chamber. There would be drawings there. My flesh began to tingle. The passage narrowed and grew shorter. We were going to have to get low to get through here. But what a reward on the other side! It felt like we were burrowing into the center of the earth.

Then I saw it.

Up ahead, through the opening, I could just make out a sort of cascade of stalagmites, and in it there appeared to be the outline of a mammoth. A mammoth! A creature from another time! I realized that I still had Mermoz's glasses on. So I took them off to see better.

That was a mistake, the biggest of my life.

Suddenly, with the dark lenses removed, the whole cave brightened and it felt like God was descending into our midst and directing my gaze toward the art. I had a sense of being in a truly magical place.

Then I dropped the glasses.

They clanked loudly on the metal walkway.

The scientist in front of me was a young woman, the one Mermoz had been teasing two days ago. The sound of the glasses hitting the metal startled her, and she turned and looked directly at me. As I rose from retrieving my shades, I glanced back at her. She gasped.

"You're not him!" she exclaimed.

The security guard was three people behind me, bringing up the rear. There was no doubt that he had heard what she said. Suddenly, I was in deep trouble. I had just two options. The first was to scurry deeper into the passage and take my chances hiding from him in the recesses of the Chauvet. I dropped that possibility instantly. I would either be lost forever or he would quickly find me. So I seized my only remaining possibility. *Run! Run back to the entrance and out of the cave!* Turn and rush past the scientists behind me and by the security guy, before they could even think about laying hold of me, then make for the door!

But the woman grabbed me, gripping my battery belt. I tore it off in one motion and dropped my panel light to the walkway. I pivoted and got past the three men behind me in a flash. Caught by surprise, as I'd hoped, they merely gaped in astonishment. I was sure that nothing remotely like this had ever happened in the Chauvet Cave.

But the guard was a good one. He was ready for me. He reached out to seize me. I ducked. His swipe knocked the helmet from my head. It sailed off and fell with a crash into the precious mineralized floor of the cave, a floor mostly untouched by humanity (and certainly by plastic hard hats) in 32,000 years! I felt terrible about that. But at this very moment it was a good thing for me. It caused the guard to stare, wide-eyed, at the helmet, stunned for a moment. It was as if he had been in charge of an historic, priceless Ming vase and I had just smashed it to smithereens.

His pause allowed me to pass him. But now I had no hat and no light. Attempting to recall exactly how the walkway went, how many steps there were upward and where they were, I rushed along the metal surface back toward the steel door, blind, praying that somehow, *somehow*, I could get to it and open it. I was imagining how many years I would get in a French jail for this. I hadn't wanted to hurt anything or anyone! I had just wanted to see the paintings! In an instant, the guard was after me.

Then I fell.

"*Voilà!*" shouted my pursuer, reaching out for me. But I kicked backward and hit him somewhere— I don't know where; it felt like his shoulder. He cried out and fell on the walkway. I heard his helmet fall off, strike the walkway and crash onto the cave floor too!

Up the first flight of steps I went in the pitch black; then I turned and raced up the next flight, thinking hard about where the stairs were. They were steep, but I timed them correctly. I took two or three strides at the landing and smashed into the door. It almost knocked me cold.

It was locked, sealed as tightly as a tomb.

Behind me, the guard was pounding up the stairs, his way lit by the beam from a scientist's helmet behind him. He was yelling at me.

"*Arrêtez! Arrêtez!*"

But then, a little woozy, I heard a faint sound outside.

There was someone on the other side of the door. I could hear him, calling a name that sounded like the security guard's. Then I heard the *ping-ping-ping-ping-ping* of the numbers being punched on the key pad out there.

Suddenly the door opened.

The man who had given us our shoes must have heard me crash into the door. An alarming sound, no doubt, and likely one he had never heard before. Perhaps he had even heard the shouting inside. He must have thought something had gone terribly wrong and that someone needed help. He was right.

I rushed past him into the blinding light, emerging from a lost world back into reality, reached down and grabbed my runners, stuffed them into my big pockets, and began racing along the pathway toward the scientists' buildings, the Pont d'Arc and freedom!

Tree branches whipped against my sleeves and my face. I had long legs, hockey and football legs, and I could run like the devil if I needed to. I needed to now, big-time.

The man who opened the door had been so stunned by my appearance that he hadn't moved at first. But when the security guard came out of the cave shouting in French, both were immediately on my tail.

I had a good head start. I wondered if it was enough. I sped downward with everything I had, twisting and turning, thinking that the two men behind me were at least in their forties and that I should be able to outrun them. I had to beat them soundly. I couldn't just slightly outpace them: I had to get far ahead, to somewhere, *anywhere*, where I could get into a car and escape, without them seeing the vehicle or its license plate. How I was going to commandeer a vehicle was another question. I ran so fast that in minutes I could see the first parking lot in the distance, beyond the vineyard.

That was when I thought of Mermoz and his getaway car. *Yes! He* would be down there, waiting for me. Surely, he would help me; surely, he wouldn't be the villain he said he could be.

But then I saw him.

He had heard the shouting and was coming up the path toward me. He had a look of anger in his eyes. He was yelling something. I couldn't tell what it was. Then it became clear. And when it did, I realized that he wasn't joking about the part of his plan that had scared me so much. He was naked except for his boxer shorts, a new wig and a goatee.

"Scoundrel!" he cried. "Scoundrel!"

For an instant, I hoped he was kidding. But his hands were stretched out toward me and the anger wasn't leaving his eyes.

Mermoz was coming at me, blocking the pathway. He was going to play this out exactly as he said. The great Mermoz was going to seize me and send me to a French jail! My chance to fulfill my grandfather's dreams, my chance to exonerate him, to impress Vanessa Lincoln, to change my life, was gone.

SIXTEEN
THE MEANING OF LIFE

Mermoz was a strong man and very sweaty and, of course, almost naked. I decided to give him a little "shake 'n' bake," which is what our number-one running back on the McKinley High Minutemen calls a move he makes on linebackers when he gets them one-on-one in open field. I gave Mermoz a little feint with my head, shoulders and hips, then spun around, putting my back to him, in order to slip by on the path. But he seemed to be blessed with some athletic ability too, because he didn't go for the move, at least not for all of it, and actually got his hands on me as I tried to slide past him. Maybe he played soccer or rugby or something. His sweaty chest was instantly glued to my back, his arms wrapped around my ribcage.

"I have you, scoundrel!" he shouted at the top of his lungs. He was projecting his voice up the hill toward the security guard and his cohort, who were barreling down toward us.

But I'd had it with Mermoz, big-time French author, artist and self-promoter extraordinaire. He was absolutely nothing like Antoine de Saint-Exupéry.

So I squirmed sideways and gave him a knee in the...uh...well, I hit him where he didn't want to be hit. Where no man ever wants to be hit. And I did it with a great deal of violence. I wasn't about to let this clown ruin everything.

"*Sacré bleu!*" he cried out, in a voice that was almost two octaves higher than his normal tone. At the same time, he released me and shot his hands toward the area I had so expertly injured. A man like Mermoz has his priorities.

My move had two perfect results. First, it incapacitated my enemy, but even more importantly, it caused him to fling himself, as dramatically as he seemed to do everything, across the path just as the other two men arrived. The collision was spectacular and accompanied by an impressive array of French curses. One sound that echoed in the gorge indicated that at least two skulls had collided. All three men lay on the path for a while, groaning and moaning, not moving.

I made the most of the opportunity. I was down the hill as if I were the fastest guy on the US Olympic track team. Going down, it almost felt like I was flying. There were times when it seemed like my feet didn't touch the ground for several yards at a time. The terrain flattened out near the vineyard, and then I was past the scientists' buildings, through the parking lot and on my way toward the other path that went toward the lot for the Pont d'Arc.

"*Arrêtez!*" I heard a voice cry out and glanced back. The security guard, the biggest and the strongest of the three men who were in pursuit of me, had recovered. In fact, he was already nearing the buildings and had spotted where I was going. It must have been the other two skulls that had smacked together.

"*Le gouvernement de la France,*" he cried, "*vous ordonne de vous ARRÊTER!!!*"

I knew that fleeing would probably make whatever they did to me even worse, but I had to take a chance. I had to gamble that I could get away. If I could just reach the next lot, perhaps I could escape. But once I was on that second path, the guard seemed to be gaining on me. He must have known the terrain very well. I was growing more frightened. How on earth would I be able to elude him! Mermoz's getaway car was probably locked and parked near the scientists' buildings. I had no means of driving out of here! I ripped off the goatee and pulled off the wig and stuffed them into my coveralls. I had to take them with me. I didn't want them to be recovered as evidence of the great crime Mermoz would be accusing me of. I was glad I hadn't given him my real name.

I reached the Pont d'Arc parking lot and stood there for a second, looking about, anxious to find some way out, *any* means that was faster than on foot. Should I actually steal a car? Should I go that far? Then I heard words that were like music to my ears.

"TAKE OFF, EH!"

The Canadians! They were at their vehicle and having some sort of a spat. Not a real one, just the sort Canucks like to have when they are teasing each other. They were arguing about something, shoving each other around. Probably about the merits of French beer, or European girls, or maybe something about hockey. I didn't know and I didn't care. They were at their car, ready to leave!

I raced up to them.

"Hey, Buffalo!" one of them called out. "Why the rush? Why the red face? Why the funky blue overalls, man?"

"USA! USA!" chanted the other one. "Run, Yankee, run!"

"Get in the car!" I cried out.

"What?"

"Get in the car! Someone is after me!"

"Dude, did you mess with someone's chick?" asked Molson.

"A car chase?" cried Maple Leaf, and instantly he was behind the wheel, Molson piling in beside him, and me diving in through the open window into their backseat.

Maple Leaf seemed to know what he was doing, or maybe he'd watched too many action movies, because he turned a smoking 360 in the parking lot, wheels squealing, and raced out of there and onto the main road.

"Away from Vallon!" I yelled. "Turn left! Toward the highway!"

He did as I said. Both of them were having a great time.

But that didn't last very long. They weren't too pleased when I told them that the authorities from the cave were after me. It took them a while to get it out of me and I didn't tell them exactly why I was being chased, but that didn't matter. They slowed the car down. That scared me. I was sure they were going to turn me in.

"I think you should get out, dude," said Maple Leaf.

"Our lips are sealed, Buffalo," said Molson, "but you gotta go."

I didn't need an invitation. Out I got. That was fine with me. We were already about ten miles down the road, and I figured that just about any of the kayakers and canoers around here, most of them young and all of them hippies and tree huggers, would give me a ride. They wouldn't know why I was standing there on the side of the road, nor would I tell them.

Still, the five minutes I waited there were excruciating. I kept expecting the security guard to come roaring along with a screaming police escort of cars. I kept waiting for the two-note blare of those creepy

French sirens. I knew that if a cop picked me up this time, he wouldn't just take me back to my hotel.

When somebody finally did stop for me, in another dilapidated old Citroën, I didn't say a word about why I was hitchhiking. I sat in the guy's car, scared out of my mind, pretending to not know a single word of French, trying to look composed, thinking about what I had done and wondering why in the world I had attempted it. Grandpa was right: it was impossible, and I never should have tried. The authorities would be asking questions back at the Pont d'Arc. They would be very wound up. This had likely never happened before. There was *no doubt* that they would be coming after me! The whole trip, this adventure that was supposed to change my life, was about to end in disaster.

The driver dropped me off in a town near the main highway that went south toward Arles and Marseille, and I quickly got myself a cab. I jumped in and sat in the back, hunched down, my breathing heavy, hoping that the police weren't following. The imagined sounds of those sirens haunted me. I still had the distinctive Chauvet Cave coveralls on. I had been seen wearing them on the side of the road. That would help them trace me.

But we got to Arles without any visible pursuit, and I headed right into my hotel, sweating despite not having moved a single muscle in the cab. I glanced toward the café just before I reached the entrance and saw Rose there. She looked over and noticed me too. She could see that my face was white, that I was terrified, and her expression showed concern.

But I didn't have time for her, for anything. I had to get to my room, throw my things into my suitcase, check out, and get my butt down to Marseille. I had to find Mom and Dad and get the heck out of France…*now!*

When I reached the room, I tore off the coveralls and Chauvet shoes and tossed them into my suitcase with the wig and goatee. I couldn't leave anything here for anyone to find. I'd burn the whole mess at home, if I ever got home. But once I had everything packed I was shaking so hard I could barely think what to do next. I felt almost paralyzed with fear. I lay down on the bed for a moment. It calmed me. For now, at least, I seemed safe. If I moved, if I went anywhere outside, I might be spotted.

I started thinking about what I had just been through. Despite all the fear, the magical interior of the cave came back to me, the feeling I had had of being in another world. And then the image of that drawing appeared before me too, that mammoth, painted onto the cascade of stalagmites. I had just glimpsed it in the distance before I had been discovered. As I thought of it, it began to overwhelm me. Someone, a human being from another time and space, more than 30,000 years ago, had created it. He had been trying to figure out his world, make sense of it by recreating an image of a small part of it. He had been making art, a magnificent and very human thing; a thing, it occurred to me, that *only* human beings do. A feeling of peace came over me. I had been *so* close to the sacred interior of the Chauvet Cave, perhaps I had been *that* close to discovering the meaning of life.

I suddenly sat bolt upright on the bed.

I had achieved what my grandfather had asked of me, hadn't I? I hadn't been all the way into the cave, but I had actually gotten inside and glimpsed an ancient drawing. Though I couldn't shake the feeling that I hadn't really discovered what he wanted me to find, I soon convinced myself that I had done enough.

I looked down at my suitcase. The last message was in there: the small white envelope. It would tell me everything! It contained my grandfather's final words to me.

I bent down, opened the suitcase and with trembling hands took the little envelope out. I sat there looking at it for a while. It felt awfully light, almost featherweight.

I opened it.

It was empty.

SEVENTEEN
IN FLIGHT

Surprisingly, my heart didn't sink. I wasn't disappointed. That was the funny thing about it. And stranger still was that I didn't know why. That empty envelope meant something to me, something very powerful. I knew it the same way I knew that my grandfather had made a mistake when he wanted to steal the Van Gogh painting, and that I had been wrong to actually take it. I couldn't find the words, but I knew it. I reached down into my suitcase and brought out the painting. I stared at it for a moment. It was beautiful. In fact, it brought tears to my eyes.

I knew what I had to do.

Five minutes later I was getting into a cab that the concierge had hailed for me outside the hotel, the painting tucked inside my jacket. No one seemed to be tailing me. Just as I was about to get in, I noticed Rose watching me at the café. I smiled at her and she smiled back.

I took the cab all the way past the Noels' old farm to Bellegarde and that busy café in the center of the village. I walked past the outdoor tables and right up to the counter. Monsieur Leblanc was there, working hard as usual. When he saw me, his face lit up.

"Monsieur Murphy!" he cried as he walked out from behind the counter and embraced me. But almost instantly, he could see that something had changed. "What is it?" he asked. "Is there something wrong?"

"No," I said, "not at all. Please take me to the Noels' house. It's very important!"

He got me there quickly. We didn't say a word in his car. He glanced down at the shape in my jacket more than once but never enquired. When we reached the Noels' place, they greeted me with big smiles and ushered me into the living room. I asked them to sit down and took out the painting.

"*C'est l'art bizarre!*" cried Yvettte. "*L'art des cochons!*"

I told them. I told them straight out. I was nervous but I didn't hesitate. I told them absolutely everything—what my grandfather had done, what I had done and what this painting was worth.

Their reaction was difficult to describe. They were angry, overjoyed and stunned at the same time. I apologized and left the painting with them.

I didn't wait for Monsieur Leblanc to drive me back to Arles. I'm not sure he would have offered anyway. I merely got up and walked out the door and then trudged the many miles back to my hotel. It scared me to be so visible by the side of the highway. I kept thinking that I would hear those sirens again and that when they picked me up this time, they would run my passport on their computers and perhaps discover that someone who looked like me was wanted in the area. But I felt I had to do this: make myself open to getting caught. It was like I had to pay a price for what I had done.

But I made it all the way back without being spotted. The sun was beginning to set by then. As I crossed the street near the hotel, I saw Rose leaving for the day after a long shift. She spied me right away and walked toward me. At first, that sort of scared me because I was so jumpy. But she was smiling at me. She came right up, put her hand on my arm and kissed me on the cheek. I felt a sensation in my chest, kind of like the one I get when I'm really close to Vanessa. I wanted to kiss Rose back, turn her face and kiss her right on the lips and linger there. Of all the girlfriends in the world, she would be the most impressive, maybe even better than Vanessa herself. Imagine having a French girlfriend, exotic and beautiful! But something stopped me. Instead of kissing Rose, I simply turned her toward me and hugged her. We embraced each other for a moment as friends, just friends, and it felt awfully good.

Ever since I had found St. Ex's rock, I had kept it buried in my suitcase. But, despite its size, I had put it in my jacket and taken it with me when I went to see the Noels. It had helped give me courage. I had held on to it tightly in my pocket as I told them what my grandfather and I had done. I reached in now, took it out and gave it to Rose. I did it almost without thinking.

"*Merci beaucoup*," I said. I didn't know why I said that, but it felt like the right thing to say. I patted her on the back and left her there, standing outside the café, looking down at the rock, gazing at its remarkable color, turning it over, about to read the inscription. I didn't even ask for her full name or phone number. I didn't want it. She was just Rose, that was good enough, and she had been my friend when I needed her. "You do not have to do this," she had said, and she had been right.

But the minute I entered the hotel lobby, fear returned. Everyone inside seemed to be eyeing me. Adrenaline coursed through my body. I rushed upstairs, finished packing my bags, checked out and got myself another cab, this one headed for Marseille. I phoned my parents and told them I was coming, that it was time to leave France. Though they answered on their cell, they were actually in their hotel room. I wondered why they weren't out somewhere, enjoying France.

They didn't argue with me. Mom had sounded so cheery when she picked up the phone, so relaxed and happy, giggling with Dad, who was in the background teasing her about something. They were disappointed that we were leaving, but after a few questions (which I put off) they seemed to accept it.

They knew that this trip was for Grandpa's requests; that was why we were in France and other things were secondary. Obviously, my call meant that either I had been successful, or I was giving up. I suppose they also relented because they were interested in what I might tell them when I got to Marseille. I knew they'd have many more questions about what I had accomplished.

At that point, I wished I had some answers.

I met them at their hotel room door. Mom opened it with a happy expression, calling out my name and moving to hug me, but when she looked at my face, she stopped. I knew I appeared anxious but didn't know how bad I looked to others. I'd been feeling so tense that I'd spent the whole cab ride to Marseille scrunched low in the backseat so my face wasn't visible to anyone passing by. The cabdriver had looked at me suspiciously and that worried me. Every siren I heard made my heart thump. And even when I'd reached the hotel, I was checking out everyone who looked at me. I'd noticed that my voice was trembling when a bellman asked me if he could help me with my suitcase.

Still, I was surprised at Mom's expression. I must have looked terrible.

"Adam, are you all right? What's happened?"

"Nothing."

"Nothing?" said Dad, getting up from his laptop at the room's desk. As he looked at me, he seemed almost as concerned as Mom.

"Everything is fine. I'll tell you later. Have you booked the flight?"

"Booked it?" asked Mom, "I thought we'd go tomorrow or the next day."

"Tomorrow or the next day!" I almost shouted at her. "We *have* to go today! Are you guys packed?"

"Today? Packed? Honey, it's ten o'clock at night! We can't leave tonight."

I had to give in. We got online and booked an early morning flight out of Lyon. For some reason, Grandpa had asked that we fly home from there. I wondered why he had insisted on that, why we couldn't just take a fast train up to Paris and then get the heck back to America, land where you didn't need to know anything but American things, land of Vanessa Lincoln. I could hardly wait to get home.

Though Mom and Dad tried mightily, they were unsuccessful at getting much out of me. We had planned to spend some time in Paris at the end of the trip,

SHANE PEACOCK

but I pleaded that I was too tired to do that now. I told them only vague things about what had happened during my assignments, saying that I'd simply done "okay." That word kind of hit me hard when I said it out loud. *Okay.* That's what I still was, or maybe worse.

They had two beds and offered to sleep in the smaller one, which was pretty funny, since it was obvious to me that they'd been sleeping in it during their holiday anyway.

I tossed and turned all night, very afraid, listening for the sirens in the streets of Marseille and sensing that all the footsteps that thundered up our hallway were coming right to our door. When I lay on my side, in the fetal position, I could hear and feel my heart beating. It really seemed like it wanted to burst from my chest. I was overwhelmed with a sense of failure too. I had tried to steal the painting, I didn't have St. Ex's rock anymore, and I had not only barely gotten into the Chauvet Cave and not truly sensed its meaning, but I had been chased from it and had become a wanted criminal. The poor Noels, so sweet and nice, likely now hated both my grand-father and me. And what would I tell Vanessa about

218

these supposedly glorious adventures? If I told her the truth, would I have any chance with her? And did having a chance with her really matter?

Only a few things calmed me, and then only partially. That hug of friendship with Rose, the feeling it had given me; the way I had felt when I gave up the rock; and the fact that I had returned the painting.

I also kept thinking about Leon. I wanted to see him, and hoped that he was doing well. I knew that if I could talk to him now, he would help me too. He would put everything into perspective. He would tell me the truth.

❖

I was the first one up in the morning. We'd set our alarm for 5:00 AM, but I'd been watching the clock like a hawk all night (I doubt I slept a wink), and I roused Mom and Dad before the buzzer even went off.

They kept trying to get more out of me while I stood at the door with my suitcase, my legs actually shaking, waiting for them to finish packing. I couldn't believe how long Mom took in the bathroom. Dad and I have this thing back home where we sit in the car waiting for her whenever we are going anywhere and joke about how long women take to get ready. (Of course, we wouldn't dare ever tell her we did that.) Now, Dad sat on one of the beds, trying to engage me in the same sort of man-to-man chat. But he couldn't raise a smile out of me. I could see that it worried him.

Lyon was a couple of hours up the road. When you go that way, you have to drive along the highway I took to Vallon, and there's a turn-off to the Ardèche that is marked prominently. I couldn't even look at it when we passed. I had been allowed to sit in the front passenger seat beside the cabbie, my parents in the back together, holding hands, smiling at each other like I hadn't seen them do in years. At least someone had gotten something out of this trip. The cabbie actually tried to engage me in conversation, but after about ten one-word responses on my part, he gave up. Mom and Dad didn't seem as worried about me during the car ride; they were kind of cooing at each other all the way to Lyon and not noticing much else. Normally, that kind of conduct on their part would have made me gag, but I didn't care. I kept my eyes focused on the road, willing the cab past the Ardèche turnoff and on to Lyon.

The airport, thank goodness, was a little south and east of the city, so we got there even sooner than I thought and didn't have to drive through too much traffic.

There was major a surprise when we got there. I couldn't believe what I saw on the sign as we approached. The place was called the *Aéroport Lyon Saint-Exupéry*!

It didn't mean anything to Mom and Dad. They just kept on whispering to each other like high-school sweethearts, not even aware that we were nearing the airport. In the midst of my fear, it made me smile. Now I knew why Grandpa had insisted on us flying out of here.

The airport itself was pretty cool-looking too. Then again, I'd come to expect nothing less from the French. A good portion of it was very long and thin, like a massive hallway, silver on the outside and with an awesome roof designed to look like it had huge slashed vents in it. Right in the middle of that long stick, a really wicked feature rose above it. It was sort of in the shape of a gigantic sail, or two sails, or an artistic interpretation of a jet plane of some sort. It was hard to describe, but it was stunning.

St. Ex would have been proud. It actually made me forget my situation for a little while. Inside, the airport was even more amazing, its ceiling rising up in a billowing crescent shape above us.

But soon I wasn't even looking at the building. My fear returned. We were near the finish line but still not there. I tried to press my parents to move as fast as they could. We marched off across the hard, gleaming marble floor, announcements echoing in the building the way they always do in airports, me very much in the lead, guiding us toward the checkout counter. We had loads of time, but I didn't care. My goal was to get through security as fast as possible. I wondered if the authorities could do anything to me once I was in the departure lounge. Was I in international territory by then? Was I back in America?

Then I heard something that sent a shiver down my spine.

"ADAM MURPHY," said a voice in English over the airport loudspeaker, "PLEASE REPORT TO THE SECURITY DESK ON THE DEPARTURES FLOOR."

EIGHTEEN

WAIT HERE

I couldn't believe it. I froze where I stood. We had
been just about to check in. We were so close. I wanted
to run.

"That's strange," said Dad.

"I wonder what they could want with you?" added
Mom.

"Adam?" said Dad. "You look awfully white.
Do you want to sit down?"

"I'll speak to the security people," said Mom.
"This must be some sort of mistake."

"NO!" I cried out.

SHANE PEACOCK

"Adam? Why are you shouting? You don't look right. I insist that you sit down," said Mom. "Why are you so pale? I'll do this for you."

"No, you won't," I said, staring right into her eyes. I had to face this. I couldn't involve my parents in my situation unless it reached the point where I absolutely had to. I was going to go over there and see if I could get out of this. The authorities had no proof. Not now. But then I remembered something. I glanced down at my bag. The coveralls were in there, and the Chauvet shoes, and Mermoz's hair. I couldn't dump them now. Security would be watching me. My heart sank.

But I walked over to the counter on my own, rolling my suitcase, my parents watching from a distance. Dad was getting on his cell, likely calling some of his connections at American Airlines.

"I am Adam Murphy," I said to the uniformed woman at the counter, who looked tough and mean. Her face was broad like a man's, her chin wide with a dimple cleft into it, a noticeable fuzz of dark hair on her cheeks.

She looked at me sternly, her mouth a straight line. "*Une minute*," she said and got up from her stool behind the counter. Then she looked back. "Stay there," she said in a low voice. Then she turned, took a few steps and opened a door behind her. She began whispering to someone, looking back at me. Then she returned to the counter.

"Wait here," she said.

I could hardly stand. I began to rehearse what I would say. I'd say I was simply staying in a hotel with my parents in Marseille and didn't know anything about Vallon-Pont-d'Arc or the Chauvet Cave, and only admit to even being in Arles if they knew about my hotel there. I was trying to convince myself that they had no way of tracing me to the Ardèche region. Then I started thinking about all the people who had seen me there—the tourist kiosk woman, the guys who gave me rides, the patisserie owner, the two Canadians and, of course, Mermoz himself. His word was likely bond in France, likely beyond bond. Then, of course, there was the evidence in my suitcase, held in my very hand at this very moment. I started thinking that my best bet was to run. Maybe I could make it into the departure—

The door behind the counter opened and a man stepped out. He was huge. He had to turn his shoulders to get through the door. He, too, was dressed in a uniform, but he also had a helmet on, as if he had been outside doing something. It looked similar to what the Nazis wore. He seemed a little out of breath. He had probably just arrived, perhaps from the Ardèche. He had something under his arm, a package. *What had I left behind?* What evidence did he have? It looked awfully small. He stared at me.

"Are you Adam Murphy?" he asked without expression.

"Yes," I said. It was barely audible.

The woman leaned toward the man and whispered in his ear. She seemed to be saying something about identification, that I must be thoroughly identified.

Now seemed like a good time to run.

Then the man smiled. "No need for identification," he said in English. "There is a note with this package, saying what you look like, sir. I had to go outside to search for this in another building. It has been here a long time. We were instructed to give it to you when your name appeared on a flight manifest. Here you go. Just sign on the line."

I signed the paper he gave me, barely able to hold the pen, scrawling my name so badly that it was almost illegible.

"But…what is this?" I managed to ask. "Who is it from?"

"What it is, I do not know, but it comes from a man named David McLean. He said in his letter that you would know him."

"Grandpa?" I said out loud and nearly fainted.

I took the package with me, unopened, through the checkout and security. Mom and Dad smiled at Grandpa's cleverness, how he set this up so that I would receive something from him almost from beyond the grave.

But what was inside the package? What was this final message?

NINETEEN
A SIMPLE SECRET

I sat in the departure lounge, staring down at the package. It felt light. But I could tell that there was something inside. This wasn't another empty envelope. Mom and Dad kept pestering me to open it. For some reason, I didn't want to. I had had enough drama and fear. Even though I still wasn't sure that I was absolutely out of danger, my heartbeat had finally slowed a little and I was enjoying that. I just wanted to put this whole thing behind me. I also didn't want my parents to be involved in any way. I wasn't looking forward to explaining what had happened, to outlining my grandfather's failures and, more importantly, my own.

This adventure, these catastrophes, were my thing, mine alone. So we sat there, them prodding me, me refusing, putting them off and telling them that I'd deal with it on the plane or when we got home.

Finally, they both went off to find the washrooms, hand in hand. Alone, I became restless and started arguing with myself. Shouldn't I open the package? Wouldn't now be a good time, while Mom and Dad weren't here? With nothing else to do, I kept mulling over the situation, glancing down at the package, wondering if I should just get it over with. If I opened it now, I wouldn't even need to tell my parents that I'd peeked inside. I looked down at my grandfather's handwriting, the way he'd elegantly written my name, his hand still steady when he wrote it. I thought of what he had said about me. "He'll never amount to much." I knew I couldn't leave the package sitting on my lap all the way to Buffalo.

So I opened it. I felt around inside. It was a book, a small one. I pulled it out—a battered copy of *The Little Prince.*

And it was *just* a copy of Saint-Exupéry's little novel, nothing else. No big deal. I knew the story.

I didn't even need to read it again. When I showed Mom and Dad, they kind of took the same approach. They tried to look interested in it, but I could tell they were disappointed. The great revelation of the contents of the mysterious package from beyond the grave was an anticlimax. And since they knew nothing at this point about Grandpa's connection to the author, that made the book even less interesting to them. They talked about how Grandpa had read it to me when I was a kid, and Mom said he'd even read it to her when *she* was little, but she didn't seem too excited. She said it was "nice" of him to give it to me and went back to holding hands with Dad, talking about how good it would be to get home.

On the flight over the Atlantic, with *The Little Prince* on my knee, I was surprised to find myself reasonably comfortable in the air, not exactly completely at ease, but not terrified either. I was in a window seat, my favorite on planes, since it helped me to look outside when turbulence started and understand that the wings weren't coming off. Dad was fast asleep in an aisle seat. Mom was beside me, smiling away, glowing at him and at me, glancing down at the book on my lap every now and then.

Able to turn my mind away from a fiery crash into the ocean from 50,000 feet, I tried to think of something positive. And when I did, I thought of Vanessa. She looked great in my head, wearing one of those sweaters and her tight jeans, her blond hair tossing in the imaginary breeze next to her locker. Wow. Then I imagined what I would say to her. It wouldn't be that hard, really. She would never know exactly what happened. All she'd know was that I went away and came back. I could tell her that it all went well. I could do that, if I were careful, without telling a single lie. The story—another of my perfect stories—began to build in my head. I could simply tell her that I found the painting and told the Noels about it, that I found the Saint-Exupéry rock and that I actually got inside the Chauvet Cave. Yes, that would work. I would impress her as someone special, a worthy son and grandson. I imagined the look in her sky-blue eyes. Would she kiss me? Would she invite me to her house? Would we become more than friends?

But Shirley kept intruding into the story. Her kind eyes, her shy smile, what she had said about liking me for who I really am. Leon Worth's comments about her came back to me again. I remembered that I still hadn't written her the postcard I'd purchased for her (or the one for Leon either), that I'd only sent her two short texts all the time I'd been away, and I felt awfully guilty. When I thought of her, I thought of Rose too. In fact, they seemed interchangeable in my mind. I didn't know whether to feel guilty or good about that. But it was Shirley's face that stayed with me, smiling at me. I was surprised at how pretty she was. In fact, there was something about her that was even more attractive than Vanessa. It came from somewhere on the other side of her beautiful eyes, somewhere inside her.

I tried to keep my mind on her and other good things and not dwell on what had happened back in France. Mom and Dad had stopped asking me questions, though I knew they'd want to know more eventually. I wondered if I'd ever have the guts to tell them exactly what Grandpa had asked me to do and exactly what I had done.

But my thoughts kept returning to Arles and the Noels and the Van Gogh, to the rock and the Cave.

I couldn't stop them. And then a funny feeling started coming over me. I kept getting this sense, a sort of happiness inside me, like I used to get on Christmas Eve as a kid when I went to bed. I couldn't explain it. Hadn't I failed miserably? But the more I thought about it, the more I wondered if I had actually succeeded. I started to think that maybe the whole trip was about one single thing: telling the Noels what my grandfather had done and having the courage to give them back the painting. Everything else—the search for the rock, the attempt to find the meaning of life (I almost laughed out loud at that for some reason), didn't matter, or at least was just a part of my grandfather's plan to get me to do what was right, both for him and for me. I wondered, for a fleeting second, if maybe he was wrong about me never amounting to much, if maybe now I had amounted to at least a little.

I hadn't won anything in France, I hadn't made any money, and I wasn't coming back a conquering hero. I was beginning to think that I didn't really want Vanessa anymore. It was Shirley I kept thinking about. Sweet Shirley, who really liked me and wanted to be not just my girlfriend but my best friend too.

I thought about all the things I valued back in America, the same things that my friends cared about: the best-looking girls, money, cars and winning at every freakin' thing we did.

I wanted to get something off my chest. I set *The Little Prince* in the pouch in the seat in front of me.

"Mom," I said, turning to her. "Grandpa once said a terrible thing about me."

She looked a little startled. But I didn't stop there. I had to tell her. I let it all out: about the last day I'd seen Grandpa, when I had overheard them talking in our house in Buffalo, when he had said that he was certain that I "would never amount to much."

She laughed.

I felt like strangling her.

"I remember that too," she finally said.

"You do?"

"Yes, quite clearly. It was a horrible thing to say."

"So, how can you laugh?"

"I'm sorry, honey, but it's kind of funny when you know the whole story."

"What do you mean? It *was* a horrible thing to say. It's bothered me ever since…a whole lot."

"But it wasn't horrible at all."

"It wasn't?"

"No, it was very sweet."

"Sweet?"

"Yes, that's another reason I remember it. He could be awfully tough on the exterior, my dad, but inside, he had a wonderful heart. He knew what mattered. And he knew what you were going through, and so do I."

"You do?"

"Yes, he knew you'd have lots of pressures on you, that you'd always strive to be everything to everybody, that that was what you were like. He knew you worried about being a worthy McLean."

"So why did he say what he said?"

"Because he understood. He loved you. He knew you would figure out what mattered in the end."

"What do you mean?"

"When he said you'd never amount to much, I gave him a very hard look. You are my little boy, you know."

I felt my face going red.

She put her hand on my knee. "*He'll never amount to much.* I actually gasped when he said that."

"So did I, Mom." I felt like I was going to cry. It was good to get this off my chest but it was awfully hard too. The memory was so horrible. "I'd just come in the door and when he said it I ran back outside."

"You shouldn't have."

"What do you mean?"

"Because that wasn't all he said. He looked at me when I gasped, as if he couldn't understand my reaction, and just kept on talking."

"He did?"

"I remember it very clearly." She smiled and tears came to her eyes. Then she imitated her amazing father speaking of me, Adam McLean Murphy, that day in Buffalo, after I ran from the house and missed every word:

"*He'll never amount to much. That might be the world's judgment of my grandson right now, but it will never be mine. The world is often wrong. He will amount to a great deal. Someday this boy will prove it.*"

I sat there, stunned. Then I had to *really* fight to hold back the tears. I couldn't cry, not in front of my mother. That's not what guys do.

A few minutes later, as I gazed out the window at the ocean far below, I realized that I was now totally and completely unafraid of being in the air. An absolute calm came over me. I hadn't needed to go into that cave to understand what mattered in life. It had been inside me all along, and Grandpa had known it.

I noticed *The Little Prince* in the pocket of the seat in front of me. I pulled it out and turned to the first page. But before I could begin, I saw something I hadn't noticed before. One of the pages was folded down. I turned to it. At the very top, someone had written something in a black marker. It was Grandpa's handwriting. *From D.M., with love*, it said. Farther down on that page he had highlighted a sentence. It came from the mouth of the Little Prince, from far up in the heavens.

"And now here is my secret, a very simple secret: It is only with the heart that one can see rightly; what is essential is invisible to the eye."

If your soul can smile, then mine did, all the way home to Buffalo.

ACKNOWLEDGMENTS

First thanks goes to Eric Walters, whose teeming mind came up with the concept for Seven (the series), of which *Last Message* is a proud member, and for placing me among such stellar company as fellow authors John Wilson, Norah McClintock, Richard Scrimger, Sigmund Brouwer and Ted Staunton. Thanks, of course, also goes to the team at Orca Book Publishers, including Andrew Wooldridge, Sarah Harvey, Dayle Sutherland, Leslie Bootle, Teresa Bubela and Kelly Laycock. I am grateful for the inspiration of some great art and artists: Vincent Van Gogh, Antoine de Saint-Exupéry and the creators of the Chauvet Cave drawings. Philip Callow's *Vincent Van Gogh: A Life*; Steven Naifeh and Gregory White Smith's *Van Gogh: The Life*; Stacy Schiff's *Saint-Exupéry: A Biography*; and Werner Herzog's beautiful film, *Cave of Forgotten Dreams*, were all essential reading and viewing.

SHANE PEACOCK is a novelist, playwright, journalist and television screenwriter. His bestselling series for young adults, The Boy Sherlock Holmes, has been published in ten countries in twelve languages and has found its way onto more than forty shortlists. To learn more about Shane and his books, go to www.shanepeacock.ca.